MW01286691

Published by BookPop Media LLC

Edition 2

ISBN 978-1-956918-06-9

23.9.26.2R

1st edition date of publication: October 30, 2021

1st edition eBook ISBN: 978-1-956918-02-1

1st edition Print ISBN: 978-1-956918-01-4

Cover design by Fay Lane (https://faylane.com/)

Symphony of Crowns and Gods Official Website:

https://www.theauthorbrian.com

JOIN BRIAN A. MENDONÇA'S EMAIL NEWSLETTER

WHY SIGN UP?

It's simple: fans on this email list get my official updates before anyone else, including any other blogs and social media websites. Here's the news you can expect:

- Upcoming releases and previews of upcoming books
- An open dialog about my author journey
- Deals and sales
- Opportunities for ARCs (Advance Reader Copies)
- Info about fantasy books from other indie authors

Sign up link:

https://theauthorbrian.com/join-brians-newsletter

Or use this QR code:

Greater Events of the World

as verified by Iris Thorne, Councilwoman
of Internal Affairs of the Second Darian Kingdom

The Human
Uprising
(Years 1-171)

Scourge of the
Dragon Slayers
(Years 171-401)

The First
Great War
(Years 441-449)

Downfall of
the First
Darian Kingdom
(Years 441-446)

Lucidian
Civil War
(Years 445-449)

Founding of
the Second
Darian Kingdom
(Year 450)

The Blooming of
All Nations
(Years 450 -   )

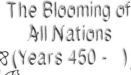

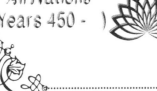

Scheduled:
Marriage
of Darian Princess
Lydia von Stonewall
and Throatian Prince
Thane Asche
(Year 474)

SOUTHEAST YAENIA

HAVENTOWN

SKY TOWER COAST

THE LOWLAND GRAVES

HILLSIDE REACH

NEW GINSTOWN

WARGONNE

GALE VILLAGE

LAST HOPE

EMIL

THE LEILA KINGDOM

STARLIGHT BEACH

LUCIDIAN ENCLAVE

WEDDING
OF THE
TORN
ROSE

SYMPHONY OF
CROWNS AND GODS
BOOK ONE

BRIAN A. MENDONÇA

1

THE PRINCESS

Kaine knelt in the mud, brown water seeping into the knees of his trousers. His calloused fingers plucked several mushrooms from the tree stump as he examined each one's quality. The forest was gently still, a perfect atmosphere for foraging, but the growl of his stomach interrupted the silence. He swallowed and sighed. The mushrooms were edible, but they were worth more to sell than to eat. Kaine could eat the mushrooms now and be full for the day, or he could sell them and eat for the rest of the month. The Darian Kingdom's capital, Last Hope, was less than a day's walk away; he planned to sell his stock there and buy himself dinner later.

He cleared the stump of its fungi, then stood. His somewhat wrinkled, sun-tanned face glanced over at the other trees for more mushrooms, but they were devoid of the types he sought. Someone else must have already come through this clearing.

Hunting down valuable mushrooms had been the least likely thing Kaine imagined himself ever doing, but it was a viable means of getting himself back on his feet. Nobody could have foreseen that the trade route across the ocean would shut down, rendering the merchant ships out of business. Though Kaine was skilled as a merchant, he was alone now—the members of the crew he'd worked with had each gone their separate ways once they'd docked for the last time. No matter what, Kaine wouldn't return home, even though he knew he could easily find a new job there. His family's name, Khalia, still left many doors open to him in the Leila Kingdom, but he'd intentionally kept them all shut since leaving his previous home behind.

He had some coins, but not enough to settle down somewhere, or even stay at an inn for longer than a week. The forests just outside the Darian Kingdom's capital were rich in flora, including valuable mushrooms. Despite the risks of encountering bandits, Kaine had nothing of value on him, so searching among the bases of the trees, alone as he was, posed little risk. If he could fill his entire satchel a few times, he'd have enough money to pay for proper lodging until he could find a stable job among the various markets in the capital. If that plan did not succeed, it could be taken as a sign he should return home after all.

As he sighed again, the first scream cut through the air—a woman's voice. Kaine drew his sword, rusted from the sea, and looked around. His heart pounded five times, then the second scream came. It was nearby. Clutching his pouch, he ran toward the sound as tree branches snapped and leaves rustled not far away.

When he reached a clearing, he froze. A severed arm in a patch of bloody grass greeted him as a creature he'd never seen before gnawed on the rest of the body. He had little time to gape at it as the young woman ran toward Kaine.

"I'm sorry!" she yelled. "I'm so sorry!"

She sprinted past Kaine and cowered behind him. The monster dropped the corpse and turned its gaze in their direction. Slowly, it shifted its four legs and moved toward them. Kaine stepped forward, and the beast stopped. With a quiet growl, it took another cautious step closer. The girl held her hands to her mouth, trying to control her hyperventilating.

Several seconds passed without either party taking the initiative in the confrontation. Kaine held his blade in front of him, maintaining eye contact with the creature's orange-colored irises. Whatever the monster was, it held a desperate hunger in its eyes. Many stories were told of monsters, but Kaine had believed none of them were real. None of them had included a beast like this either—something between a giant wolf and an eagle. Its body was furry, wild, and oily black, yet feathers covered its wings. Kaine made a mental note to avoid the sharp, bird-like talons protruding from its wolf-like paws.

The monster jolted forward. Kaine took a quick step backward and grounded himself while the young woman trembled behind him. Swinging his sword, he roared and broadened his chest. He knew little about fending against a wild animal, other than that some bears and mountain lions were fearful of loud noises. His long-term familiarity with sword-play was useless against something like this. Blades had been indispensable when he traveled at sea and fought the occasional pirate, but there was a signifi-cant difference between battling a two-legged crea-ture and one that had four. This was a fight he could not win if they engaged head-to-head. Intimidating it away would be the safest action.

The strange beast yelled back at them, a sound midway between a howl and a screech. It lowered its body and then leaped toward them for its attack. As it almost became airborne, its wings flapped, but it didn't seem to know its limits; its body was too heavy to fly and crashed straight down into the mud. Seizing the opportunity, Kaine shoved his blade through the beast's skull. He leaned onto the hilt of his sword, pressing with the full weight of his body until a cracking noise came from beneath him.

Black blood spattered over him as the creature gave a brief yelp and collapsed into the wet dirt. As the corpse landed, Kaine lost his balance and fell backward. He had gotten lucky; with no armor, a single strike from the monster would have killed him.

"Are you okay?" the young woman said in a single exhale.

"What in Asura's ass was that thing?" Kaine rolled over and lifted himself off the ground. He wiped some sludge from his emerald-colored shirt, gawking at the beast's body.

"Are you okay?" she asked again. He estimated she was a little under half his age, but no older than twenty years. Likely a commoner who lived in the slums of the capital, she wore a plain brown tunic. Mud covered her face and much of everything she wore, but it wasn't clear whether it was normal for her or because of the encounter with the monster.

"I'm fine," he said, wiping the sweat from his forehead, "but where did the monster come from? It seemed strong, but... stupid, like it's never tried flying before. I don't—but it has wings. So why couldn't it fly? None of it makes sense."

The young woman reached behind her copper

hair and scratched her neck. "I-I don't know. It all happened so fast."

He couldn't blame her for her nervousness; it was possible the monster wasn't the only one of its kind. Still, where had it come from?

"That's okay," Kaine said. "Are there any more of them around?"

"No."

Kaine remained in awe that he had killed a monster—an actual monster! "I thought such creatures only existed in fairy tales. Where did you find it?"

"It found me." The young woman settled onto a nearby log. "But it's my fault."

"How so?"

"I ran away from home."

Raising an eyebrow, Kaine asked, "Did you argue with someone?"

"No," the young woman responded, gulping as she stared at the ground. "I'm Princess Lydia von Stonewall, and I'm supposed to get married this week." Chances were she was a servant to the princess, not the actual Darian Princess Lydia von Stonewall.

Kaine gaped at her, examining her tunic again. "Truly now?"

"Yes, truly. Why would you doubt me?"

"It just so happens that I've saved Princess Lydia

from a monster in the forest? It seems a bit too much like a typical children's fantasy story, doesn't it?"

As he chuckled, the young woman grinned back at him. "Whether it's believable doesn't change the fact that it's true. We're lucky to be alive."

"Yes, I suppose so." His day was getting more peculiar by the minute. "So, what are you doing out here in the woods so soon before your wedding?"

He wanted to comment on her clothing and test her further, but she continued speaking. "Long story short, I wanted to skip my arranged marriage, so I ran away. I'm truly her. My servant and I came out into the woods, but… she died. You saw."

She folded her arms and crossed her ankles. Kaine, finally calming down from the battle, sat next to her. While at sea, he'd heard that the Darian king had arranged for his daughter's marriage to a foreign prince, but there were no other details. The girl seemed uneasy, but there didn't seem to be a motive for her to lie about being the princess—in fact, there were plenty more reasons she should have kept such information secret. However, if she were lying, the truth would inevitably reveal itself.

"I'm guessing your father gave you no say in the matter of marrying the Throatian prince," Kaine concluded.

The princess winced. "That's correct."

He glanced down at his shirt, trying to wipe away

some mud he'd overlooked during his first examination of his clothing. "I understand not wanting to go through with your wedding, but rushing out into this forest was reckless. The roads outside the Darian capital aren't safe. Dangerous people roam around—people who would rob you or do worse. And apparently, we have monsters too."

"I know, but I'm certain there won't be any more of them," Lydia said. "I'm certain the monster was alone."

Kaine shrugged at her naivety. It was better that they be cautious. "Where were you trying to go? Or did you merely want some space from your father?"

Lydia sighed, pulling her arms closer to her chest. "Gale Village was my destination. I wanted to get away from Serenity Keep, somewhere where my father couldn't find me before the ceremony. It was childish to run away. I knew that, but what else could I do? I had to buy myself time to figure all this out."

"For that, I'm not sure," Kaine admitted. "Who in all of Yaenia could be an expert on these kinds of things?"

Lydia leaned her head back and embraced the sunlight that permeated the trees. "What happened there with the monster changed my perspective. My handmaiden is dead because of me. I'll proceed with the wedding. If that monster had turned me into its lunch, everyone would have blamed me for abandoning my duty as a princess. I was stupid and put myself and others in danger. I'm sorry for causing you trouble."

"The wedding wasn't your idea in the first place. Anxiety is natural and expected," Kaine encouraged. "I'm sure nobody blames you for fearing it."

"Of course not." Her manner of speaking and willingness to share so many details suggested she truly was the princess. Returning her to the king would be best—Kaine could sell the mushrooms he'd collected in the capital that same evening and venture back into the forest the next morning.

"So, we should help you get home, then. I'll help you return to Serenity Keep and then I'll be out of your way."

"Out of my way?" Lydia asked, tilting her head sideways.

"Yes," Kaine said. "Once you're home, you'll need to prepare for your wedding. As for me, I'd prefer to avoid meeting anyone at the castle, if I can help it."

"Why's that?"

"I haven't conversed with royalty or upper-class families in a very long time," Kaine said. "I'm not up to date on the latest formalities and such. It would be better if I didn't risk embarrassing you."

"Don't be silly. I will make sure you receive a reward. As you said, many other people would have taken advantage of me in this vulnerable situation. I insist you deserve something, Lord or Sir…?"

"I'm Kaine Khalia," he answered. "And I'm no Lord or Sir. I'm just a common merchant. Rumor has it this forest grows valuable medicinal materials, and I was foraging for them."

"You have medicine?" Lydia asked. "Can you heal my leg? I got a rash earlier from a bush, I think. It doesn't hurt much, but it is stinging a bit."

With trembling fingers, she lifted the hem of her long tunic dress. Her calf shone maroon, purple veins protruding from the infection.

"How long has it been like that?" Kaine exclaimed.

"Maybe an hour or so."

"We need to leave," he urged. "Now."

"Why?"

"You've got a Mourning Bear rash," he said. "Nothing I have on me will heal that. We need a leaf ointment. Someone at Serenity Keep will have what will work. Can you still walk?"

Lydia's forehead crinkled. "I didn't realize it was serious. It's fine—I can walk. Which direction is the castle?"

"It's that way," Kaine said, gesturing northward. "We're only a few hours from your home and should be able to reach it by nightfall, provided we don't encounter any more monsters. As long as we get you home soon, there's no risk of permanent damage to your leg."

"It sounds bad. Are you sure there's enough time?"

"Yes. Provided that we make it before too deep into the evening, you needn't panic."

She took one more look at her leg, then met his concerned gaze. "I see. Thank you, Kaine Khalia."

The two of them stood up from the log and moved outward, back toward the outskirts of the forest. The main road would provide safer passage than weaving through the trees. Kaine had many questions left unanswered, but it didn't seem right to prod the princess about them so soon, especially now that she had her rash to worry about.

Ten minutes down the path, Lydia spoke up. "So, Kaine, you are a trader?" she asked, adjusting the rings on her left hand. There were four of them, one on each finger, and all shone in different colors. They seemed expensive—even for belonging to a princess. Encapsulated in the prettiest silver bands Kaine had ever seen, every one of the jewels was bright and clear.

"Yes, I worked on a ship until about a week ago. We exported various foods and spices from the Darian Kingdom to the Throatian Kingdom." After five days of solitude, it was refreshing to converse with someone.

She tilted her head curiously. "It seems interesting to travel so much. Did it pay well too? Why'd you stop working there?"

"We were able to scrape by week-to-week, but ever since the Throatian Kingdom closed its trade port, business has dwindled," Kaine said. "My captain ended up letting us all go and selling his ship. With our primary route shut down, it was too expensive to stay in the water. None of it was profitable anymore. That's why I ventured out here to gather some medicinal materials. They'll sell well in Last Hope."

"That's odd. Wouldn't closing their ports be bad for their island's economy?"

"Their country is becoming more independent from ours. They supposedly discovered how to use magic."

Lydia lowered her gaze and resumed staring at her rings. "I thought only Lucidian people could do magic, right? How can Throatians use it too?"

Something rustled in the nearby bushes. Kaine instinctively reached for his sword, but by the time his fingers grasped the handle, a squirrel rushed out from the greenery and continued its way to the other side of the road. The quietness resumed, but he couldn't help but keep his guard up in case there were other monsters.

"I have yet to witness any Throatian magic

myself, so it remains a mystery," he said. "There are plenty of rumors, but nobody knows anything for sure. The Throatians are a very reclusive people. Aside from business, I'm not familiar with anything about their culture."

"You never tried getting to know any of them? Wouldn't it have been good for trade?"

"I never had the chance," Kaine said, staring into the nearby trees. "They didn't allow foreigners past the gates of White Boar's Landing, plus they use their own language. The only Common Tongue they know is business speech. It's all scripted conversations—I don't really understand anything about their people."

"Me neither," Lydia said. "Yet I'm supposed to marry the Throatian prince and join his family. I've heard they even worship another god, different from Asura."

"It's a tough position for you," Kaine said.

"You're also in a hard spot. I'll make sure my father finds you a new job."

Kaine's ears went red. "You needn't give me any reward. There'll always be something else for me to trade in the future. Besides, I couldn't just stand by and watch that monster attack you."

"Of course not," Lydia said, thoughtfully stroking the stone of the ring resting on her index finger.

They passed an apple tree, and Kaine climbed up

to shake some fruit from its branches. He cut one of the fruits into quarters with his knife and held it out for the princess.

"Thank you," she said, taking the apple, yet still staring at her ring as they continued walking. "You saved me, but I am curious about you. Where did you learn to fight with a sword?"

Kaine frowned as he sliced a second apple. He hoped Lydia was asking about his sword training merely out of politeness, without paying too much attention to his response. Still, from what he'd observed so far, she seemed more authentic compared to most other nobles he'd encountered. Perhaps she didn't intend to be judgemental of him if he revealed his previous affiliations.

"Don't be afraid, Kaine," the princess urged. "I'm certain there's nothing too embarrassing lurking in your past. Give yourself more credit. What's your story? You haven't been a merchant your whole life. I can tell by the way you talk and present yourself."

For years, he'd kept his life from before his trading days bottled up. He often mulled over his past decisions and their consequences, questioning if he had made the right choices. His decisions had led him, in one way or another, to the forest that day. Now next to him walked a young woman—a princess, no less—who just wanted to get to know the stranger who'd saved her. She deserved that much, but the thought of revealing too much about himself knotted his stomach. He dared a glance at her, and her kind eyes looked back at him with no judgment. A surface-level summary would do. Maybe that would be enough to satisfy her curiosity.

"Fine. But only if my princess commands it."

She laughed and elevated her chin. "I do."

"Okay then, here it goes." Kaine sighed with a forced grin. He wiped his hands, now sticky from the apple's juices, on the sides of his trousers. "I was born a noble in the Leila Kingdom, destined to grow up and become a knight for Queen Blanche. I found traveling on ships and trading to be more exciting, so I renounced my future there and made my own way. The decision disappointed my family, but I was happy."

She took a moment to process his story before speaking again. "You made an interesting choice. You lost a lot of friends when you went through with it, didn't you?"

Kaine blinked twice, then retreated his gaze toward the trees. A thin, white mist had enveloped their surroundings. The air made breathing easier, even though it concealed the farther reaches of the path. "Yes, most of my oldest friends and I drifted apart, though there are a few acquaintances I have at home. I consider visiting them often, but—"

"But home doesn't really feel like home anymore

since you left?" Lydia finished his sentence. It was uncanny how effortlessly she seemed to understand his deeper feelings.

"Right," he said. "After I went to sea, I lost touch with almost everyone."

"Sometimes, it is better to have no friends at all than a collection of superficial ones," Lydia commented. Her perception of his feelings was astounding, almost unnatural. To most people, the thought of being a princess meant someone could have anything they'd ever wanted. Like Kaine, perhaps Lydia too had realized that money and power alone couldn't acquire genuine companions and happiness.

"Princess Lydia, if you don't mind me asking, why were you going through these dangerous woods? This isn't the way to Gale Village." They were currently south of where they should have been.

"Oh, I must have forgotten how to get there. I've never traveled without my father before. We used to visit my mother when I was younger."

Kaine knew of Gale Village but hadn't yet ventured to the remote town in the far east. Since Lydia wasn't carrying anything with her, she seemed unaware that the journey there was too far to under-take without provisions. He held his tongue and avoided criticizing her. "What's it like?"

"Clouds and fog float above lava-filled canyons against a background of quietly exploding volcanoes. It's so peaceful from far away. There's no noise from markets or endless parades of people begging for my attention. In Gale Village, I can rest among the grassy fields near the cliffs and read books in peace."

"While Gale Village sounds relaxing," Kaine ventured, "have you ever visited Starlight Beach? It's in the southern part of the kingdom—about a week away from Last Hope. You would enjoy the sands and ocean. There are also many shops, restaurants, and bars that entertain the students at the university. You'd like those."

"Maybe so," Lydia said. "But I prefer the quiet."

Kaine felt his face warm from his lack of attention. "My apologies, Princess Lydia. I heard you, but I wasn't considering. I'm—"

"It's okay."

They walked in silence for a few minutes, neither one of them looking at the other.

"I haven't been outside the capital very much," the princess explained. "The Leila Kingdom and Gale Village are the only places in the Darian Kingdom I've been, besides Last Hope, of course."

Normally, Kaine would have corrected someone's inaccurate terminology, but he knew that doing so would appear arrogant to the princess.

17

Most Darian citizens even considered the Leila Kingdom part of the Darian Kingdom, no different from any other place in the land. Because of the arrangements of territorial lines, one would assume the Leila Kingdom somehow belonged to the Darian Kingdom. The fact was that the Leila Kingdom was its own entity, despite being surrounded by Darian lands.

At the Lucidian Civil War's end, nearly twenty-five years ago, Ether von Stonewall promised Blanche Voussoir her own area within the future Darian Kingdom if she'd help him secure the south-eastern areas of the Yaenian continent. Though Blanche made good on hcr promise to support Ether, she vastly underestimated how many bodies she'd lose by doing it. At the war's conclusion, she only had a small town's worth of survivors left to lead, and so demanded that Ether recognize her earned reward as an entirely separate kingdom instead.

"My people need an opportunity for rebirth. We can't let our culture die with our casualties," Blanche had supposedly declared. Insistent that Ether von Stonewall accept her new terms, she secured the queenship of a village-sized territory in the south-eastern area of the Yaenian continent. Lodged between forests and mineral-rich mountains, there was plenty of room for her kingdom's future growth. For several years, including to the present, the Leila Kingdom would have to grow as the younger sister to the empire Ether von Stonewall was building for himself. The circumstances of the two kingdoms' foundations led to national pride within the Leilan population—and so they were highly assertive about reminding others of their independence from the Darians. As for Princess Lydia, she'd probably learned a different version of the story stemming from her father's perspective.

Kaine snapped out of his reminiscing and then refocused, settling his eyes on the road ahead.

"Perhaps I've only seen the extremes of my father's lands," Lydia continued. "Gale Village is serene and there are no crowds. My father used to take me there to visit my mom's grave. She's buried there near the top of a mountain."

"Oh, that's right—your mother. She passed away."

"During my younger sister's birth," Lydia added. "It was a heartbreaking decision for her, choosing between herself and Kira. I've learned to accept it."

"It must have been difficult," Kaine said.

"Thankfully, my father, brother, and sister are still with me. They're everything to me. Do you have any siblings?"

"No, I don't," Kaine said with a wry smirk. "And that disappointed my family. I had a chance for a bright future serving the Leilan Queen, but I didn't want it. My parents resented me for disrupting our family honor. From a high-born to a commoner… My father never forgave me."

Lydia nodded, playing with her ring some more. "I understand. Parents' expectations are sometimes too inflexible for their children to grow in a different direction. Your parents passed away already, haven't they?"

Kaine's mouth dropped open, stunned. "Yes," he replied. "It was years ago, and I didn't make it in time. I didn't even get the news until months after the funeral—I was out at sea." He wondered, how had she guessed?

"It's okay, you don't have to say more. Don't let the past weigh you down. I can see that you're a good man, Kaine Khalia."

"A good man? I'm not sure. I see myself as just average."

"No, I'm certain of it," Lydia affirmed, her face alight. "Believe me, I know."

2

THE PROPOSAL

Half an hour after Kaine returned Princess Lydia to her castle, an apothecary provided the antidote for her poisonous rash. Positive she was no longer in danger from the venom, the servants quickly swept her away to meet in private with her father. Meanwhile, Kaine was instructed to wait in the audience chamber until summoned to the throne room. Everyone seemed to be in a massive rush—most likely for the upcoming wedding.

He paced back and forth through the small room, staring down at his mud-stained clothes. Under normal circumstances, his clothing, particularly his silky green shirt—shiny, elegant, and completed with golden buttons—would have been appropriate for meeting the king, had it not been covered in dried mud, sweat, and monster blood. He'd been wearing a matching pointed cap earlier, but had lost and forgotten about it during the fight. Paired with his dark brown pants and satchel, his outfit was comfortable and presentable. However, his attire was suitable for a trader ready to make a sale, but not so much for a princess's protector.

Now, Kaine looked no different from a stable keeper who'd recently finished his daily duties. He'd left a change of clothes—his more practical outfit—back in Starlight Beach, but that was days away from the capital where he now stood. Before leaving, he'd imagined meeting someone along the road who could give him work, so he'd selected his better outfit just in case. That was his mistake, trying to save room in his satchel for more mushrooms. Even if he'd had the coins, there was no time to shop for clean linens.

The doorway leading into the throne room creaked open and a tall, dark-skinned man in an elegant jade-colored robe burst through it. He appeared high-born, but at the moment, mostly nervous. Despite the sweat and overall rush that the man seemed to be in, Kaine interjected.

"Excuse me, sir," Kaine called out, causing the man to freeze and glare back at him.

"Who are you?" He looked Kaine up and down, clearly judging his filthy clothing. "Are you supposed to be here? You're not with the Throatians."

"I'm Kaine Khalia. I brought Lydia—I mean, Princess Lydia—back from the forest."

The man's scowl disappeared. "Oh, Sir Khalia! That explains the mud. I understand now. Please accept my apologies, and thank you for rescuing the princess. You've really saved the day for us, you know. The Throatians arrived at the castle not long ago. It would have been terrible if they'd come, but there wasn't a princess for Prince Thane to marry! The king will reward you—"

"Thank you," Kaine interrupted. "Actually, I need help with something. You're not a servant, but perhaps you can help me find clean clothes? We both know that my current attire isn't suitable for meeting the king."

"Ah, I see," the green-robed man replied. "You needn't worry about your clothing. The people beyond this door know who you are and what you've done for the kingdom. You could be wearing rags and they'd still praise you. Nevertheless, I'll ensure you're brought something suitable."

"Thank you," Kaine said. "And may I know who you are?"

"I'm Councilman Merdel, Master of Foreign Relations," he replied. "I apologize for my bluntness, but I need to go check on our Throatian guests.

Someone'll bring you a fresh set of linens soon, I guarantee it."

He strode off from the audience chamber toward the other areas of the castle. After a few quiet minutes, a servant delivered the change of clothes Merdel had promised. She led Kaine over to a small room and he changed into a maroon-colored tunic paired with onyx-colored leggings. She took his dirty clothes and satchel and promised to return them cleaned later that evening.

"Are the accommodations to your liking, Sir Khalia?" the attendant asked as she escorted him back to the audience chamber.

"A perfect fit," Kaine said. The clothing was far fancier than anything he'd ever owned, and he was afraid to soil it somehow.

They reached the audience chamber where another servant was already waiting for them.

"Thank goodness you're back," the young man said. "Please come. The king and princess await."

Passing through the massive open wooden doorways, Kaine's eyes immediately locked onto the king's throne. He'd heard about the Darian Kingdom's throne before, but seeing it in person, he realized the rumors had failed to capture its genuine beauty. Supposedly, only hand-crafted diamonds imported from the Silent Deserts made up the royal chair, but it appeared more like glass—transparent and beautiful. Kaine couldn't fathom how the artisans had created something so smooth and pure.

Ahead of him, Princess Lydia stood by her father. Other men and women, whom Kaine guessed were the Darian council members, observed from his left. He kept his eyes averted, as their stares made him nervous. The subtle observations and judgments from nobles were among the many reasons Kaine had renounced his high-born status. He grunted quietly as his knee thudded against the stone floor. Holding his bow, he waited for King Ether von Stonewall to speak.

"Welcome, Kaine Khalia of the Leila Kingdom," the king said. "You represented the Leila Kingdom's loyalty today by returning my firstborn daughter to me. She told me of how you defeated the strange beast that attacked her. Thus, you have my greatest thanks—not just as a king, but also as a father. She informed me you did not desire coin nor reward. Is this true?"

"I need no compensation, my king," Kaine said, getting to his feet. "I did what was right, and that alone brought me honor."

The council members exchanged glances. Were they obligated to attend this meeting, or did they relish scrutinizing every newcomer to the throne room? The one named Merdel was absent from their group.

The king laughed. "You're well-spoken!" He turned to the council members and pointed back at him. "Kaine Khalia pretends to be a commoner, but he still remembers how to play the game of filling a noble's ear with pleasantries. I like this man already! Lydia, you said he was a merchant, correct?"

Lydia had been fiddling with one of her rings again. Upon hearing her name, she dropped her hands to her sides and looked back up at her father.

"Kaine is a sailing trader who is soon to be without a job, Father. He found me by chance while foraging for mushrooms to trade." Her azure eyes met Kaine's as she tried to contain her smile. Kaine bowed his head further so as not to draw attention to their connection.

The king nodded. "How inconvenient for you. Tell me, Kaine Khalia of the Leila Kingdom, why did you abandon your upper-class privileges? I had one of my council members look up your family's name and learned all about your connections to Queen Blanche. Serving her would have given you a promising future, yet you refused. Why?"

Kaine balked. He was uneasy about discussing his

past in front of strangers who might not fully understand it. The king wouldn't want a monologue of his
various reasons for leaving, either. So, what else
could he say?

"Never mind," the king announced before he
could craft a proper response. In the court, Kaine's
silence was palpable. "With the Throatian Kingdom's
ports closing, might you consider rejoining the
world of the high-born?"

It was as Lydia promised; the king was going to
offer him a role. Even if it was a minor position,
serving a King was far from simple. There were so
many rules, regulations, and formalities to remember, both written and unwritten. Life in the upper
class had its share of difficulties.

"Um—yes, my King," Kaine lied. Outright
refusing the king would be rude, but if they negoti-
ated first, then he could politely decline. "I would
consider returning."

"Perfect! Here's my proposal," the king replied.
"You know I have three children; Lydia is getting
married later this week, but Xander and Kira are
only twelve and ten years old. They need a new
retainer. Their last one unexpectedly fell ill and
passed away."

"Pardon me, your highness, but what is a retainer?" Kaine asked. "I'm not sure we have them in the
Leila Kingdom, or perhaps we use a different term."

The king chuckled. "My children will require more attention while they are younger, but as they grow older, you'll train them in swordplay, good morals, and protect them if need be. Princess Lydia will explain the day-to-day tasks better than I. You will take a vow and swear loyalty to my family, and that oath will forever bind us."

Kaine's heart skipped a beat. "That's a major responsibility." he acknowledged, aware that accepting the offer would require him to spend more time with the prince and princess than almost anyone else. Lydia must have vouched for him strongly if the king was willing to trust his other two children with someone so far removed from high society. "Why me, though?" He ran his fingers through his brown, but graying, hair. "I mean, I'm honored, my King… but am I the right choice? You barely know me."

"My daughter insists you are worthy and persuaded me to agree. The monster killed the two handmaidens who ran away with Lydia. Their deaths are a reminder that I need to keep someone nearby who can protect my children, not just serve them."

"Two handmaidens?" Kaine blurted. There could have only been one handmaiden unless the other somehow escaped. In the heat of the moment, there wasn't enough time for the monster to have eaten two people. "Forgive me, but I thought there was only one person with Lydia."

Lydia's face flushed red as she darted her attention to her father and then back to Kaine. She quietly bowed her head. "Sorry for the confusion. There were indeed two."

"I see. Please pardon my mistake." He assumed the princess felt guilty and hadn't wanted to admit the full consequences of her wandering in the forest. Yet, something didn't add up—there had only been one body in the forest's clearing where he'd battled the monster. Perhaps something else had happened to the other handmaiden before Lydia met the monster in the woods. The most likely case was bandits. Perhaps one of Lydia's servants had given herself up as a distraction so that Lydia and her second escort could escape. There wasn't time to ponder more on that thought now though—Kaine was in the king's and princess's presence, so it was best to keep the conversation flowing and avoid stalling for too long. "You have my condolences, Princess Lydia. I'm sure your two handmaidens served you well."

Ether von Stonewall cleared his throat. "So, now you see why a blade guarding my children could have changed the outcome. Danger is unpredictable, but we could have reduced the chances of bloodshed. I've sent my guards into the forest to sweep for additional monsters, but that doesn't change how vulnerable Lydia was earlier today. That's why I want you there in the future."

"I understand your needs, my king," Kaine said, taking note of Ether's frequent glances at Lydia. "But why not simply send some troops as escorts? They'd be better protection than I as a single bodyguard. I'm decent enough with a sword, but I'm no knight."

The king adjusted himself in his giant crystal throne and gave a light nod to his council members.

"Kaine, this is going to sound trifling, but typical guards are too impersonal," Ether said. "Yes, I stereotype, but I want someone who's truly dedicated to my family and who'll swear the oath and stick to it no matter what happens in the future. This is more than a job."

"And what makes you believe I'm the sort of person who's looking for more than just a job?" Kaine asked.

The king grinned, revealing a small set of dimples hidden amongst the edges of his graying beard. "Lydia claims she's not the first princess you've rescued. She told me you once saved Queen Blanche's life, when the two of you were younger. Is it true?"

A knot formed in Kaine's stomach. It was true, but he'd never told Lydia that story. There was no way she could know that a younger Kaine had killed another boy while protecting his queen. For over a decade, he had kept his mouth shut about the accident, and he trusted that Queen Blanche did the same. It was their darkest secret, and Lydia's awareness of the incident was both mysterious and unnerving.

"Perhaps," Kaine said, feeling sweat trickling down his palms. Things were adding up in ways that made little sense.

"You have a history of saving princesses and are modest about it, exactly as Lydia said," Ether von Stonewall insisted. "I know of nobody else with that kind of record. That's why I choose you."

Kaine gave the king a stiff bow of his head. "Thank you."

"Princess Lydia is the most beautiful rose in all the Darian Kingdom," the king said, beaming at his daughter. "Despite the unusual situation of her escape, she's bright and has an excellent sense of character."

"I completely agree; though I haven't known her very long, I can also sense she has a noble character."

"So, we're back to you understanding my position as her father, then," Ether von Stonewall continued. "I demand someone I can trust with my youngest children. Someone like you. You'll have everything you desire as payment, including a home here in the castle."

Kaine's jaw tightened before he could answer. The king's proposal was a rare opportunity and a chance at a stable life, yet something else was amiss. A monster fight, a princess who seemed to know everything about him, and an offer for a prestigious role from the king all in one day was too considerable to ignore. He needed to talk to Lydia in private and learn how she knew so much about him.

"Your faith honors me," he said. "I know I keep asking this, but I still don't understand how you could trust a stranger with your children so easily."

"You're correct that I don't trust easily. However, I can trust swiftly when I recognize certain key qualities in a person," Ether von Stonewall said. "Being a leader in the war required it. Calculated leaps of faith were also abundant when I was forming our kingdom from ashes. Kaine, you can learn a lot about someone's integrity if you examine their actions when they think nobody else is watching."

He paused, considering Lydia's persistence, which hinted at the offer being less optional than it seemed. Regardless of their reasoning, a job with the king was better than scavenging around the forest for mushrooms, spices, and herbs. Here in the castle, he wouldn't need to worry about his next meal.

"Thank you," he said. "However, I'm uncertain about my readiness to reenter high society, let alone settle down in the Darian Kingdom."

"So, you would prefer mushroom picking for the rest of your life?" Ether inquired, his tone suggesting a mix of jest and annoyance. "What bothered you enough to where you'd retreat from the Leila Kingdom to the sea?"

Kaine stared at his feet, avoiding the court's gaze. He couldn't maintain his childhood friendships. The birthrights of being born in the upper class contained many perks, including his family's network of well-situated friends. For years, Kaine enjoyed taking part in their circles, but as decades went by, each party slowly chipped away at him. It may have been a coincidence, or perhaps he lacked the conversational skills, but every encounter drained his energy a bit more. Everyone had their tales, their jokes, their wit—against which Kaine's list of accomplishments and goals seemed boring in comparison. Years went by and despite everyone becoming busier in adulthood, each gathering reminded him how much he'd drifted from his original path. Eventually, his self-inflicted alienation became too much, and leaving it all behind was easier than staying.

"Father, I don't think Kaine wishes to state his reasonings," Lydia said. "But Kaine, will you do this for me? This is my brother and sister we're talking about. You can make such a difference for them."

Though the life of a merchant was simpler,

picking mushrooms in the forest was a short-term solution, not a lifestyle. Accepting the king's offer would be a suitable path for the immediate future. If Kaine changed his mind and quit later, it would surprise nobody who already knew him well enough.

At last, he yielded. "If it's the wish of my king and my princess, then I accept your offer."

"Well done!" the king declared. He turned to his daughter. "I'm impressed with him so far, Lydia. Your knack for sensing character remains spot on. I'm going to miss you after you move to the Throatian Kingdom."

Lydia's eyes shifted around the room—from her father to the council members, then back to her father—before she cleared her throat. "Yes, I'm sorry again about running away. I just wanted to have some time to think and to talk to Mom. It won't happen again."

Her father lifted his hand to silence her, then pulled it back down to rest on his lap. "No need to apologize. I put too much pressure on you. Marrying someone neither of us knows is burdensome enough as it is. I'm praying to Asura he will be an honorable man."

Kaine understood the king's desperation to form an alliance. Politics surrounded everything about the upcoming wedding, and the situation was delicate for everyone involved. He empathized with Lydia, but there was little he could think of right now that would help her. For the moment, Kaine stood in silence, remaining neutral. Who was this Throatian prince she was destined to marry?

"I wish that too." The princess bade them farewell and left. King Ether von Stonewall then redirected his attention back to Kaine.

"My apologies for the tension. Lydia and I are going to meet the family soon," the king said with a pensive grin. "Anyway, I'll have you start your new role once the wedding is over. There are many formalities, oaths, and ceremonial chores to do. There just isn't time right now. With all the wedding preparations, everything else is on hold."

"I understand," Kaine said. "With the ceremony fast approaching, every minute counts. Rest assured, I look forward to serving you."

"Speaking of the ceremony, I've got one more thing for you. Attend the rehearsal dinner tomorrow night and the wedding the morning after. Thank you for everything, Kaine Khalia."

NO SOONER HAD KAINE LEFT THE THRONE ROOM, HE found a woman waiting for him in the lobby.

"Greetings, Kaine Khalia," she called out to him in a raspy voice. "My name is Bridgette Frey. I'm the Darian council member in charge of finance and the Kingdom's economy."

Kaine nodded as he studied the many wrinkles on the elderly woman's face. "It's a pleasure to meet you, Councilwoman Frey. I hope you didn't need to stand a long time for me out here."

"I was. But first I must ask you... did you accept King von Stonewall's proposal?"

Kaine smiled weakly—the reality of his recent decision hadn't fully set in yet. "It was a surprise, but yes, I accepted. I didn't expect to be offered a role such as this."

"The king doesn't offer such roles lightly," Bridgette said. "The timing was right, and your background is appropriate. You won't regret your choice —I've been with the von Stonewall family since the beginning and they take excellent care of everyone in their house. In fact, that's why I'm here—your key." She reached into a dark leather satchel at her waist and held out a small piece of bronze for him.

"A key to what?"

"Your bedchamber, of course. You'll live here in Serenity Keep from now on."

Although the concept made sense, it marked a

drastic departure from his recent past when he'd slept under the forest trees and stars. Everything was moving fast, and things seemed different from how they'd been in the Leila Kingdom. "It strikes me as odd that the council member tasked with finances is also in charge of issuing keys."

Bridgette grinned, handing it over. "It loosely falls under the category of economy, my other domain. When our kingdom was founded, we divided up our daily roles and responsibilities so that everything happening in Serenity Keep must go through the council. Councilmen Ofred, our Master of Agriculture, even presides over the kitchens here."

It seemed like a lot of bureaucracy and bottle-necks in the way of getting things done. Still, as long as Kaine got on the council's good side, the members would hopefully serve more as allies than road-blocks to him in the future. "That's quite interest-ing," he said through his teeth as he held up the key. "Thank you for this—I look forward to staying here and serving the Darian Kingdom to the best of my abilities."

"Well said, Kaine Khalia. You've apparently remembered everything about living in the upper class." Once again, she delved into her satchel, but this time removed a smaller coin purse. "This too, is yours."

He shook his head. "I already told King von

Stonewall I don't want a reward for what happened in the forest."

Bridgette chuckled. "Or… perhaps you haven't remembered everything from your time in the Leila Kingdom, after all. These coins are the advance for your month's allowance, minus your costs for clothing."

"Oh?" He'd thought the clothes given to him were out of courtesy, not that he'd have to pay for them out of pocket. Without a doubt, they were costly. Nevertheless, the weight of the bag told him he still had more money than he would have made by selling the mushrooms.

"For tomorrow night's rehearsal dinner and the wedding ceremony itself," Bridgette clarified, "you're expected to attend both events, and the outfits you'll wear for each are being prepared as we speak. We've commissioned a very skilled tailor who's handling everything from Lydia's dress to the shoes Prince Thane will wear. She's exceptional at her trade—the council's outfits are also being custom designed. You'll get to keep the clothing afterward, but you must pay for them from your advance. Tomorrow morning, you're to have any adjustments you need made."

With a forced smile, Kaine reluctantly accepted the coin purse from Bridgette's outstretched, wrinkled hands. Something about this exchange felt like a scam. He wished she had simply given him the money without mentioning that it had already been used to pay for the clothes. Though he had more coins than he did at the start of the day, the knowledge that some had already been spent without his input left a sour taste in his mouth.

"I'm sure the wedding will be great, and all the people attending well-dressed." He gave a light bow. "Thank you, Councilwoman Frey and, again, it is a pleasure to meet you."

HIS BEDCHAMBER BROUGHT BACK MEMORIES OF HIS former home in the Leila Kingdom, the place where he had grown up. His wooden bed's headboard bore carvings of several animals among various trees. At the forest's center, a large sun dominated the horizon, its rays spreading outward toward the outer edges. His mattress was twice as thick as any he'd ever slept on, stuffed with probably a hundred birds' worth of feathers. Crimson pillows, decorated with golden embroideries, were stacked neatly on the top of the bed. He also had three blankets of various thicknesses to accommodate every season. Across the room, a desk for writing, an armoire for his clothing, and a cozy fireplace adorned the opposite wall.

Spread evenly throughout the room were paintings of knights with whom Kaine wasn't familiar—most likely they were Darian heroes from the previous war, perhaps even former friends of King Ether von Stonewall. His windows, hung with red drapes that matched the armchair by the fireplace, overlooked a small courtyard with a pink tree. The room reminded him how much he'd missed out on while he'd chosen to bunk with his former crew members at sea.

Kaine rested peacefully during his first night in Serenity Keep. At sunrise the next morning, a servant roamed the halls outside, ringing a loud bell to awaken everyone living on his floor. Kaine groaned from his bed. A few more minutes of sleep would have been nice—he had, after all, slayed a monster the previous day. He pushed the covers away and got himself dressed so he could visit the tailor as promised.

Downstairs, he entered a small library where the wedding tailor had temporarily set up her workstation. Various dresses and shirts lined most of the room's perimeter, staged upon a collection of mannequins. Some pieces were yet to have sleeves, buttons, sashes, or seams attached, while others stood completed, waiting for their turn. In the center of it all was a large, vertical mirror enclosed within a heavy, rustic bronze frame. Despite the growing collection of wedding attire filling every inch of the room, the tailor herself was nowhere in sight.

Considering it was still early, he thought about returning later. The tailor was probably eating breakfast or hadn't started her day yet. Contemplating how much longer to wait, he paced about the room, perusing each of the dresses and suits lining the walls. As he was about to leave, a pair of footsteps echoed nearby out in the hallway. Two women were talking—one whose voice was familiar.

"This shouldn't take too long, right?" Lydia said. A moment later, the princess, along with another young woman, appeared in the room's entryway.

"Good morning, Princess," Kaine said. "How are your wedding preparations going so far?"

She quickly curtsied, then straightened her violet-colored dress. "Everything's happening so fast now—I can't believe the wedding is tomorrow."

"At least the rash on your leg is better now, right?"

The princess smiled. "Today would be very different for me if you hadn't returned me to the castle so quickly yesterday."

"So, this is Kaine Khalia?" the other young woman next to her said. She wore an elegant, shiny

41

tan dress that complimented her fair white skin. "He's exactly as I imagined. Perfect."

Warmth crept into Kaine's face. He couldn't help but notice she hadn't averted her gaze since she'd entered the room. "I'm happy to meet your expectations. And you are…?"

"Here for your sizing, of course," the tailor replied with a smile, skipping the introduction.

"Of course." Taken aback, Kaine glanced over at the princess. "Bridgette Frey told me to come here this morning. If now's not a good time, I can return later. Your wedding dress should have the priority."

Despite his assumptions about Lydia's purpose for being there, none of the dresses seemed to be hers. White or red dresses were the traditional color of a bride, but all the ones throughout the room sported of shades of juniper or walnut. He hoped the tailor had already begun crafting whatever Lydia would wear the next day.

"I've nearly finished Lydia's dress—only a few adjustments remain to make it perfect," the tailor said, answering his question before he could ask it aloud. "Let me take care of your clothing first while you're already here, Kaine."

He waved his hand in protest. "I shouldn't skip the line ahead of the princess. Let me come back another time." Leading with his right foot, he retreated toward the door.

"It's fine," Lydia insisted. "In fact, I'm glad we could cross paths again now before the wedding. Everything since you brought me back here has been a blur. This feels like the first chance I've had all week to breathe."

"Besides," the tailor added, "it's thanks to you that Lydia is safely back with us. Without the Rose of the Darian Kingdom, there would be no wedding."

"If you both agree, then I suppose I have no choice." Kaine locked eyes with the tailor, whose own were sea blue. "What should I do now?"

The young woman pointed over to the mirror toward the back of the room. "Stand there. You'll try on a few shirts and then I'll fit them to you." She made her way over to a mannequin and removed a deep green shirt with a golden trim from it. As the tailor busied herself with the shirt on her workbench, Lydia accompanied Kaine to the mirror.

"I met the prince for the first time last night," she said. "His family too. Everything's going to be okay, I think. All my fears about the arranged marriage were for nothing. There really wasn't a need for me to have run away—I should have given this a fair chance from the start."

Her words resonated within him. His reintroduction into high society would be gradual, progressing step by step, until he familiarized himself with the layout of the Darian Kingdom. Like Kaine, Lydia had deliberately abandoned her birthright, but she'd quickly re-assumed her responsibilities. Had her close encounter with death revitalized her willingness to serve the Darian Kingdom? For him, his declining situation, coupled with the convenience of Ether von Stonewall's proposition, was too tempting to pass up.

Kaine offered her a warm, broad smile, sensing a change in her since the previous day. "It's great everything is coming together nicely for you. What were your impressions of the Throatian royal family?"

"There's a—um—a slight language issue. Between us, I'm having some trouble understanding their accents when they speak quickly. They mean well, though," Lydia said. "My father is happy—the Throatians all seem eager to unite themselves with the Darian Kingdom. Prince Thane seems nice too."

The tailor approached Kaine, holding the dark green shirt for him to try on. "Go ahead, remove your top."

"It's not proper for me to undress in front of the princess," Kaine commented. "I shouldn't become indecent."

Lydia giggled. "Kaine, in a few nights, I'll be married—including everything that comes with it. I think I can handle seeing a man without his shirt."

Without uttering another word, Kaine took off

the brown linen tunic he had on. As the cold air of the room brushed his chest, the tailor cleared her throat. "Those scars aren't from yesterday, are they?" She was referring to the various pink lines spread across his back.

"I used to be a merchant," Kaine said as she placed the new shirt over him and started taking measurements. "The trouble with sailing and trading for a living is sometimes you run into pirates or slavers… Sometimes you get captured too—especially around the Silent Deserts. Nothing we couldn't handle, though."

"That's terrible!" the tailor exclaimed. "How did you manage to escape?"

Lydia didn't seem surprised by the news. "Sir Khalia always finds a way."

Kaine laughed. "You're giving me too much credit."

"Faking a fight with your partner to get the guard to come over and break it up was clever," the princess said. "Then you both overpowered him and escaped." She was correct, but it was another story he hadn't told her and impossible for her to have known.

"The only one clever here is you, my Princess," Kaine said as he fastened the second topmost button on his shirt. "How do you know all these stories about me that we haven't talked about before?"

The tailor glanced at them both as she swept her blonde hair away from her fair, white face. She quickly turned her attention back to Kaine's shirt, judging its fit.

"You told me on the way back from the forest, remember?"

No, he hadn't. It was clear she was hesitant to reveal how she knew. Still, Kaine wanted to know the truth about how Lydia knew so much.

"Are you sure? I don't recall."

"Um—yes, you did," the princess said. "Or maybe I heard it from Iris Thorne… It's her job to know those kinds of things."

The tailor lightly tugged on the bottom edge of his shirt, signaling with her palm for him to remove it. "Perhaps the princess grows weary from all the wedding preparations happening around her. Your history is most intriguing, though, Kaine Khalia. I hope we can meet again in the future."

He gaped at her in disbelief. "We're done already?"

"I completed your measurements. Someone will drop the finished clothes off to your bedchamber later today before the rehearsal dinner," the tailor said.

As he was pulling his brown tunic back over his head, he heard Lydia say, "Yes, I suppose I am weary from the week. Please pardon my lapse in memory."

As if a lack of memory was the problem… Lydia seemed to remember things she had no way of knowing.

Once he was done redressing, the tailor extended her hand toward the doorway. He had seemingly overstayed his welcome. "Now if you'll excuse the princess and I, we have a lot to discuss before the wedding…"

3

THE THROATIAN PRINCE

T he smell of roasted chicken filled the throne room, though plates weren't on the table yet. Kaine sat alone, fiddling nervously with the white lace tablecloth at his table. He wasn't sure why the king had invited him to the rehearsal dinner. He assumed everyone else there held family blood, some important position in the kingdom, or a role in the ceremony. Kaine was none of them and knew nobody else present. Unless the king had invited him merely as a gesture of good-will, Kaine's presence that night seemed somewhat unnecessary.

From what he'd observed so far, the king struck a strange balance between formality and nonchalance with his subjects. He had a habit of directly addressing his servants, sometimes even making light-hearted jokes with them. Likewise, some staff members appeared close enough to Ether to where friendship replaced formalities. Kaine didn't know the history of the Darian Kingdom in the finest detail, but he suspected such relationships were the backbone of how Ether von Stonewall became king at the end of the war and the beginning of their kingdom's founding.

Rising from his diamond throne, he escorted his daughter down the nearby stairs to where servants had arranged more dinner tables, covered with plates and glasses. The castle at Last Hope was very old and lacked a Great Hall like the one back home in the Leila Kingdom.

While Kaine was half-thankful for his upcoming new job with the Darians, he empathized with Lydia's situation. The Throatian prince to whom she was engaged could be any kind of character. It wasn't fair to promise her to someone she'd never met, and it seemed even her father didn't know the family very well. Arranged marriages were rare within the Yaenian continent. Only across the sea in the Silent Deserts were such agreements commonplace and—to make matters worse—they usually coincided with slave-related business trans-actions. The concept of binding two people together against their wills made Kaine's stomach lurch. What could Lydia do if, upon getting to know him better, she decided she didn't like him after all?

"Hurry up, hurry up, please," King Ether commanded his servants. They shuffled around, carrying various flowers, plates, and wine barrels. "When the Throatian royalty arrives, it's our time to impress! This is the first time their family has visited our capital, so it's essential that everything—and I mean everything—goes perfectly. Even though it's a rehearsal dinner, treat it like it's the actual event."

Instead of assigning the event's various duties to a steward or servant, the king seemed to enjoy directly handling the finer logistical details himself. He scanned the throne room, peering at all the gathered Darian nobles and servants and counting on his fingers. "Pay attention because there are many details for tomorrow. I don't want anyone to seem like they don't know what's going on!" He looked to his left, where the princess was standing, then continued. "After all the guests sit down at these tables, the priest will begin his opening remarks. Music will play as the Throatian royal family walks down the middle aisle and stands in front of the throne…"

By then, Kaine had lost interest. Wedding events were typically formulaic and predictable. Even the most unique ceremonies bore significant similarities with other ones. He didn't need to hear the step-by-step overview of everything, so his attention drifted away… until the king started talking about something Kaine had not heard of before.

"—and then Lydia and her new husband will make the Everlasting Wish. Once the Everlasting Wish is complete, the marriage is official, and dinner will begin!"

The nobles clapped and cheered as a meek Lydia, now dressed in a semi-formal cerulean gown, stepped forward. "Thank you, everyone. I am excited to meet my soon-to-be-husband. I haven't decided on my Everlasting Wish yet, but I promise it will be something great." Whatever the Everlasting Wish was, something about it sounded ominous, yet hopeful. Perhaps there would be something unique about the event after all.

A servant approached the king and whispered into his ear. Ether von Stonewall's eyes widened, then he caught himself and smiled. "The Throatian royal family has arrived. I will be back in a moment, then we'll begin."

As the king strode towards the exit, several servants carrying barrels of wine dodged out of his way. Meanwhile, Kaine focused on Lydia. She was conversing with a Darian council member, exchanging laughs. A trio of women entered and began singing a soothing opera to the slow, yet uplifting melody of a single violin. Kaine closed his eyes and listened, unable to understand the lyrics of the old Yaenian song they were singing. Just as the anxiety of being at the party finally began to melt away, someone grabbed Kaine's shoulder.

"You've got a lot of nerve, crawling back out of the salt water and sand, you flopping sea dog," a gruff, familiar voice whispered into his ear. Kaine turned around, and a brown-bearded man let out a bellowing laugh.

"Eisenbern!" Kaine exclaimed. "What are you doing here?"

"Patrolling and making sure that little crabs like you don't cause trouble," Eisenbern chuckled. As he laughed, his purple tinted armor shook along with his body.

"Where's Queen Blanche?"

His old friend feigned a cough. "Not going to ask how I've been all these years or tell me why you're here in the Darian capital instead of the Leila Kingdom? I'm hurt." He gave Kaine a light punch on the shoulder.

"Come on," Kaine replied. "You can tell I've been doing well because I made it out here."

Eisenbern let out a genuine laugh and sat down next to him. "You're as forthcoming as always. I should have called you a sea turtle, not a sea dog! Lame jokes aside, Queen Blanche is sick. Nothing serious, so don't worry about her. It's just too much trouble to travel all the way here under those circumstances. I'm here representing the Leila Kingdom on her behalf. Did I mention that I'm now her right-hand man? Rank One of the Purple Guard!"

It was the most powerful title someone could hold besides the crown itself—it was no wonder Eisenbern was representing their kingdom. Despite having no other family left alive, Queen Blanche once told Kaine her intentions of never marrying or bearing heirs. Rather than endorsing a society ruled by bloodlines, she upheld the old ways of selecting a new king: the rite of the Lion's Den. The decision went against every one of her advisor's warnings, but Blanche was the most stubborn woman Kaine had ever met.

"They insist that it's irresponsible for me to set the law this way, but there's a reasoning for my decree. One day, when I keel over and the crows and worms take my body, I want there to be an epic battle over my grave," Blanche had explained to Kaine long ago. "The last one standing will fight tooth and nail to maintain our kingdom's independence. Whoever has the guts to succeed or die for my seat is the one I want ruling our kingdom when I'm gone."

Because anyone could take part in the borrowed, now-extinct tradition from the Darian Kingdom,

Blanche ran her kingdom differently from other lands. Most notably, her Purple Guard doubled as her council within the official hierarchy. Her protectors needed skills with the mind and blade along with their proven loyalty, for if anyone assassinated her, they'd have a direct and legal way to the Leilan Throne. Eisenbern's new role came with a lot of weight, a responsibility Kaine knew he wouldn't have been able to bear himself.

"That's great," Kaine said. "Well, not about the Queen, but your new rank. I'm glad you got the spot instead of me."

Though he was pleased for his friend's accomplishment, seeing the position filled by someone he knew was borderline uncomfortable. Kaine's parents would have held it against him if they were still alive, without a doubt.

"Thank you." Eisenbern itched his thick beard. "At first, I didn't want to come here. My guard duties are more important than my diplomatic ones while she's sick. I told her this."

Kaine raised his eyebrows. "And she still sent you here despite that?"

"Yes, for sizing up the Throatian Kingdom. Military scouting. This wedding binds the Throatians to the Leila Kingdom too, in a way. I'm supposed to be checking how strong of allies the Throatians will make. They're from a small island after all."

"And Blanche wanted a first-hand account of the Throatians' magic too, I imagine," Kaine finished.

"Exactly," Eisenbern said. "So, what are you doing now? And how in Asura's ass did you get invited to the rehearsal dinner?"

Kaine cleared his throat. "As of a week ago, I was recently an unemployed ship worker. Now I am the retainer of the younger Darian prince and princess."

"How in the black sands did you get promoted to that job? You weren't even born in Last Hope. You're Leilan."

"To cut a long story short, my rescue of Princess Lydia in the woods apparently qualified me for the job."

Eisenbern laughed again. He was slurring his words a bit, and Kaine wondered if he was drunk. In the past, they had consumed copious amounts of alcohol together, but Kaine had quit drinking sometime after their last meeting. "So, you're the one they are calling The Boring Knight of the Woods? No way!"

Kaine squinted. "Excuse me... the Boring Knight?"

"There's already so many stories and songs about heroic knights saving their princesses from beasts and creatures in the woods," Eisenbern said. "People are tired of hearing the same old tales. Now, thanks to some loose-lipped servants, you're known as the

Boring Knight because your story is so much like the other stories. Not everyone believes the part about the monster, you know."

Kaine prayed his reputation wouldn't spread very far or last very long. The last thing he needed when starting his new role was an unprofessional title.

"If I die before you, make sure that's not what the bards call me in the songs," he grumbled. "I didn't think my deed would become so widespread."

"You know how it goes. Nobody can stop the rumors, if they're interesting. Servants always leak the secrets and gossip they hear. Besides, everyone in the kingdom loves the princess—the Rose of the Darian Kingdom, as they call her. But tell me," Eisenbern leaned in conspiratorially, "was the monster real?"

Kaine nodded grimly. "I could only kill it because it made a mistake. It tried to fly, but its wings couldn't support its weight."

His friend let out a loud whistle. "What did the monster look like? Was it anything like the artists of the Golden Kingdom imagined? Scaly and snakelike?"

Kaine's neck went stiff as he tried to remember what Eisenbern was referencing.

"Are you referring to Sunken Seagonne? The island that sank after an earthquake?"

"Yeah."

"I've actually never read their lore," Kaine admitted, "but the monster was more beast-like than reptilian. The king sent guards into the forests to find more of them, if they are there. I'm sure they've brought the corpse back to study if you want to see it yourself."

"Come on, Kaine," Eisenbern said. "What did it look like? You can't just hold out on me!"

The wooden doors creaked open, and several people stood at the entrance. A priest walked in first, down the aisle, and toward the crystal throne.

"Actually, you'll have to save that story for later," Eisenbern whispered with a frown. "Looks like the Throatians are here."

THE THROATIAN ROYAL FAMILY WAITED IN THE doorway, examining the intricacies of the golden embroidered silk curtains hanging down the walls. They were all bundled in silky iron-colored tunics. At well over six feet tall, the Throatian king and queen towered over Ether von Stonewall's servants, who were ushering them into the throne room.

"Welcome, everyone," the servant host announced when he reached the dais where King

Ether sat on his throne. "Tonight, I welcome the Throatian Kingdom's royal family. They've traveled across the ocean from their homeland to grace us with their presence tonight and for the wedding. Everyone, please pay your respects to the Throatian king, Harkbin Asche!"

The crowd cheered as Harkbin advanced, brandishing a hefty metal scepter in his hand—broader than Kaine's lean yet muscular arm. He wondered whether it was the scepter that allowed Harkbin to use his magic.

"And, of course, the Throatian Kingdom's queen, Urith Asche!"

A large scar stretched from her right eyebrow down to her clavicle. Kaine guessed she had previously fought in a war or been in a fight. Urith and her husband probably held nothing back when settling disagreements.

Eisenbern elbowed Kaine lightly. "Those names sound like they choked on something."

"Yeah," Kaine replied. "But the names are fitting for how tall and tough looking they are."

Eisenbern nodded as the announcer continued.

"Finally, we have for you... the man of the evening, the future husband of Princess Lydia von Stonewall... Prince Thane Asche!"

The Throatian prince stepped forth. Thane, taller than the average Darian man, did not match the overwhelming stature of his parents, nor did he mirror their brutishness. Instead, he radiated confidence, holding his chin high. His ghostly-white skin provided a stark contrast to his dark and untamed hair.

"Greetings, Kingdom of Daria," Thane addressed the crowd. "It is an honor to visit your lands and celebrate our union of peoples."

His Common Tongue accent, though harsh, bore an almost musical rhythm. Kaine's previous travels to White Boar's Landing as a merchant had familiarized his ears to the fierceness of Throatian language, but no matter how much of it he'd heard, their speech always sounded like they were singing angrily at each other. Thane's accent was much the same.

Despite the intensity in his voice, Thane appeared sincere in his desire to unite the Darians and Throatians. "The Darian Kingdom was born at the sunset of war," he said, drawing his speech to a close. "Today, it grows stronger, greater than ever before. When my father arranged my marriage to Princess Lydia, I understood the importance of promises. Love and unity between two people build the bridge between their kingdoms. For that, I am grateful to serve my part."

Even though he was somewhere in his early or mid-twenties, Thane already seemed mature enough to lead his people in the future. The crowd cheered as Thane gave a bow. His father, Harkbin, took to the stage next, also wielding a tone of subtle intensity. "Our country is a simple one," the Throatian king said. "For generations, we've limited our contact with the outside world, choosing to minimize our culture only to what's necessary. Mindfulness, loyalty to our god, inner peace, and remembering those we've lost to time are our values. Though our island is small, our dedication has no limit. Tomorrow, we join our worlds together for the greater good of all!"

Last, Urith stepped forward. "I have little to say except our alliance will speak for itself as it matures. My son is the most suitable husband a woman can find, strong in both character and mind. May he and Lydia rise together as one."

Ether von Stonewall offered them a beaming smile. "Though they are new to our lands, they are clearly fine people, as you can see. We welcome the Asche family to our home with open arms!"

THE TWO ROYAL FAMILIES SPENT THE BETTER PART OF the next hour stepping through motions and proceedings—practice for the morning's wedding. As the guests observed, servants delivered white wine to everyone, filling their glasses. When they approached Kaine's table, he quietly shook his head and waved away the offered glass.

"My apologies, sir," the servant said. "We've only got the white wine tonight. We'll have both reds and whites tomorrow."

"Oh, sorry," Kaine said. "I mean—I don't drink alcohol."

"Asura's ass," Eisenbern bellowed. "What are you trying to pull? You're usually the one to out-drink a horse."

Kaine gave him a nonchalant smile. "I don't think I can anymore. I gave up drinking not long after I went to sea. Mostly survived on fermented milks and coconut water when possible."

The servant handed the glass over to Eisenbern instead, but before he could leave to the next table, the leader of the Purple Guard told him to wait.

"One glass of wine won't make you drunk," he said to Kaine. "You fought a monster earlier. Don't tell me you needn't clean that off."

Kaine sighed. Regardless of its effects on the past, alcohol always helped make conversations in the present easier. Besides, out of all his former drinking buddies, Eisenbern was the least of them likely to instigate that they get into trouble. "All right. Just one glass then, but only for old time's sake."

"For old time's sake!" Eisenbern asked the servant to pour another drink for Kaine. Merrily, he handed the crystal over to him and clanged their glasses together.

Kaine sipped the drink and his taste buds danced with the fizzy essence of pears, apples, and oak wood. It was sweet, yet crisp, and perfect for the occasion. Eisenbern was right that one glass of it wouldn't make him drunk, but he was crazy for thinking it would be enough alcohol to help someone unwind. Of all the times to cave in, now was the most justified. Kaine had earned it.

"Besides Queen Blanche's illness, is there any other news from the Leila Kingdom?" he asked. "I bet your new role keeps you busy."

Eisenbern moved his head from side to side, cracking his neck. "To be honest, it's easier than I expected. The training I went through to prepare for war, espionage, and politics nearly scared me away from putting my name forward as a candidate. I expected the job's pressures and responsibilities to knock me on my ass, but it turned out not to be so bad once I actually started. My days usually boil down to me going where Blanche tells me to go and telling someone what she wants me to say. I'm a glorified messenger, armed with a sword in case anyone disagrees with the word."

Kaine gaped at him. "It can't be that easy. You have the duty of protecting the queen."

Eisenbern took a large gulp, finishing his glass. "I do, but how many days out of the year is there a blade at her throat? No, I just need to be ready to spring into action, any day, any time. The rest is easy."

A servant promptly returned and refilled Eisenbern's wine. After returning the glass to him, the servant held his hand out toward Kaine. "More for you too, sir?"

Kaine looked down and realized he'd finished his drink already, too. The wine was more like fruit-infused water than true alcohol. One more glass wouldn't cause any trouble.

"Sure," he responded automatically. Once the servant refilled his glass, he took another sip. "So, you'd almost say being in the Purple Guard is boring then?"

"As if it were the Boring Knight's place to lecture me on what's interesting. Ha!" Eisenbern said, lightly slapping Kaine's shoulder. "Nah, we sometimes have interesting situations come up that need investigating. The lower-ranking members of the City Guard usually do the legwork, but I stay abreast of what they're doing."

"Such as?"

"Have you ever heard of the People's Army?" Eisenbern asked.

Kaine rested his arm on the table. "Scammers, right? I'd heard stories of them operating at the ports of Starlight Beach."

"They've spread to the Leila Kingdom now, too."

"I see." Kaine took another drink, then a deep breath. "Scammers and swindlers seem to be getting smarter by the day. I hope you manage to apprehend them."

"We'll get them, someday," Eisenbern promised.

The room fell quiet as the royal families approached the platform in front of the throne again. King Ether raised his goblet. "And now that we're done with the ceremonial plans, the Dancing of the Sun and Moon begins!" He took a sip, and the crowd of guests followed suit.

Starting on opposite sides of the room, Lydia and Thane began their solo dances, gradually rotating in circles toward each other. Kaine watched as the two of them spun and circled until they reached the center. Lydia appeared to have rehearsed her dance beforehand; she circled confidently and smoothly. Prince Thane seemed rigid and forced, as though he'd memorized the steps but not practiced. As they slowly danced for the audience to adore, Lydia brought her thumb to the ring on her index finger and closed her eyes.

Lydia and Thane separated, starting the next phase of the Sun and Moon dance. The princess met her father, and Thane his mother. For a few moments, they danced separately within their own families, after which Lydia joined the Throatian Queen in a paired dance. Thane and King Ether retired to the sidelines as Lydia and Urith went through various unfamiliar hand motions, twists, and turns. Kaine noticed Lydia repeatedly touching the jewel on her ring with her thumb at every opportunity.

Soon, it was King Harkbin's turn to dance with Lydia. Being significantly taller, it took him a moment to adjust for their height difference. Lydia wound up standing on her toes as Harkbin hunched his neck and back, but they still couldn't see each other eye to eye. They danced the minimally expected amount, and then Lydia and Thane joined again. They circled a few more times in the middle of the throne room before turning to the audience and bowing. Lydia's face had turned pale and was glistening with sweat. Kaine wondered if it was because of nerves, but the copious perspiration suddenly dripping down her forehead suggested she might have a fever.

Unaware of his daughter's sudden shift in

temperature, King Ether von Stonewall stepped into the center of the room once more to make another announcement.

"Thank you for watching the practice round of the Dance of the Sun and Moon! Now, the second round of ceremonial vows and Everlasting Wish would happen, but I think we need not practice those. I don't know about you, but I am eager to begin tonight's feast. The sooner we finish tonight, the sooner tomorrow will come. Now, lo-and-behold, the best chickens in Yaenia!"

He bowed his head in silence for a moment to pray to Asura, then raised his arms, and a flurry of servants carried in plates of whole cooked chickens for each of the guests. Kaine's eyes widened as the metal plate landed with a loud thud on the table before him.

"This chicken is almost as large as a turkey!" Kaine exclaimed as he gawked at Eisenbern's similarly oversized meal.

"There'll be bigger ones tomorrow, sir," the servant bragged.

"I can't believe it." Kaine surveyed the bird from all angles, grappling with where to start on such a colossal piece of meat. He enjoyed chicken, but this was beyond anything he'd ever eaten.

"Gotta say, Last Hope has the Leila Kingdom defeated on chicken farming," Eisenbern commented. "This bird could easily feed an entire family!" He took a large bite, leaving grease and flecks of meat stuck in his mustache. "I guess tonight I'll be eating a family's worth of food!"

Kaine took his first bite. The chicken was juicy, hot, and flavorful; it may have been the best chicken in the world. He glanced back toward Eisenbern. "I wonder what they fed these chickens to make them taste so good and grow so large?"

"I'm not sure, but from the looks of it, you might have a second chicken for dessert." Eisenbern pointed a leg toward the main table where the royal families were eating. "Look over there."

The Throatian king, with a frown, pointed at his plate. Kaine caught the end of his sentence through the bustle. "…which is why we don't cook our food before eating them."

"All your meat?" King Ether von Stonewall asked, mouth lingering open and displaying half-eaten bird. "Y-you eat all your meat raw?"

"Correct," Urith replied. "The blood needs sharing with our god before we can eat it. It's part of our religion."

"By all means," the Darian King said, "I will arrange for two live chickens to be brought to you for your rites. Know that we of the Darian Kingdom will respect your religion, even though I am not yet personally familiar with it."

Prince Thane nodded. "It is quite fortunate your country is so open-minded. This wedding will be beneficial to all our causes. Please have a third chicken brought in for me."

"Of course!" King Ether von Stonewall said. "You teach us how to do things your way, and we will accommodate. You are our guests and our allies!"

A moment later, Kaine watched a trembling servant bring in a small wooden cage, which contained three plump, live chickens. Were they really about to slaughter them right there in front of everyone? Harkbin grabbed one by the neck and held a blade to its face.

"You must present the knife and say these words before you kill each chicken: Sheiaa Kaaduul. Once you say this, we consider the offering made. Sheiaa Kaaduul!"

Harkbin sliced open the chicken's neck and raised it, spilling blood into his empty cup. He then cut into his hand, letting his blood drip into the cup as well. Next, he lifted the cup for all to see and swirled it.

"Normally, we would leave the cup at an altar overnight," Harkbin said. "The mixing of the blood and surrendering it to our god symbolizes shared life, spirit, and suffering. Suffering is inevitable in life for everyone, and death is imminent. The next morning, we consider the blood consumed by our god. Blood grants our god his power and through it, our god blesses us in return."

Kaine observed Lydia's face growing even paler, her arms twitching slightly. Harkbin's greasy fingers plucked the feathers from the bloody chicken and then he began eating the raw meat. Kaine grimaced at the sight, noting the nervous glances exchanged among council members.

"Um—it's an exquisite offering. I see its value," King Ether said, his eyebrows betraying his surprise. He gulped down some of his wine. "Thank you for demonstrating the common ritual of your culture. In the Darian Kingdom's religion, we simply pray to our god Asura before our meals."

Asura was the official crown-supported god of the Darian Kingdom. While the von Stonewall family allowed smaller religions to exist in the kingdom, they mostly didn't acknowledge them. It surprised Kaine that Ether would allow his daughter to marry into a family with a different religion.

Eisenbern nudged Kaine's elbow. "Eating raw meat will make them sick. Don't they know?"

"Maybe they've done it so long already that it no longer matters?" Kaine suggested. "Or magic?"

His eyes drifted back to Lydia, who, he realized, was staring back at him. With their gazes locked, she subtly jerked her head to her left. Kaine downed the rest of his drink and walked in the direction she'd indicated, to a small table where servants were refilling drinks.

"Excuse me," Kaine addressed the servant at the minibar, "May I get a refill, please?"

"Oh, my goodness, Lord Khalia!" the servant exclaimed. He grabbed Kaine's empty cup. "I apologize. I didn't see your empty glass, or I would have come over to your table and refilled it again myself."

There was no time to correct the servant's misunderstanding about his title. Lydia had already reached his side. "Kaine could use the extra walking, given the glorious feast we are enjoying tonight."

"My princess," the servant gasped. "I'm so sorry you had to walk over here for a refill too." He refilled her wineglass, trembling and splattering the liquid as he poured it.

"No need to apologize, sir," Lydia said.

Once the servant scuttled off to tend to the other tables, she stepped closer to Kaine and brought her head next to his ear. "Meet me in the graveyard outside the castle tonight at midnight. Don't tell anyone. Please."

"Are you okay?" Kaine asked. "You appear exhausted, as if you've journeyed to the black sands of Tornaa and back."

"I'm better for now… I think," she said. "Let's talk more about it later."

As the attendant returned to their vicinity, Kaine

let out a fake laugh. "Why yes, you're right. The chickens look like they've been eating other chickens."

Lydia giggled nervously, curtsied to him, then walked back to the royal family's table without saying another word.

"What was so funny over there?" Eisenbern asked, as Kaine sat down again.

"The princess wanted to thank me again for the monster. She also said everyone is going to be too sleepy to enjoy the wedding tomorrow because of the chicken tonight."

"That's so true," Eisenbern laughed. "Between the excessively large poultry and the wine, half of us will undoubtedly snooze until midday tomorrow."

Taking a sip from his latest glass of wine, Kaine felt the room sway as if it were back on a ship at sea. "It's certainly possible."

King Ether stood from his table and gathered everyone's attention again. "People of the Darian and Throatian Kingdoms, my daughter has some words to say to you all. Ladies and gentlemen, here's Lydia, my eldest daughter and the Rose of the Darian Kingdom."

The princess stood from her chair, holding her wineglass. Her azure eyes shifted around the room, and while her free hand trembled, she forced a smile.

"Thank you, everyone, for coming tonight," Lydia

said. "The most important day of my life is tomorrow. Tonight is a preview of the great joy we can expect. As many of you heard, I ran away from home because of my fear and uncertainty about what this marriage meant for me. Returning home, I've spent these past few days in deep reflection about my upcoming nuptials and what it means for all of us. I've realized that this wedding is not just about how I feel or what I want, it's also about serving you."

The crowd clapped and cheered. Lydia continued her speech, though her voice shook.

"That said, I've learned that some love comes naturally, while we build other love from scratch. I am excited to begin the journey, regardless. Joining the Asche royal family and binding our two nations together is what's best for everyone. For now, please continue enjoying your meal, and I look forward to seeing you back here tomorrow at sunrise."

The rehearsal dinner continued for another hour as Kaine and Eisenbern soon switched from drinking wine to beers. Looking at the stacked tankards and empty glasses, he couldn't tell how many of them were his and how many were Eisenbern's. As the event started winding down, a man joined them at their table. It took Kaine a moment to realize that it was none other than Prince Thane.

"Hello there," the Throatian prince said. "I presume one of you is Lord Khalia?"

"Yes, sir," Eisenbern said. He pointed his fork at Kaine. "That's him there: Kaine Khalia, the Boring Knight!"

"You have my thanks, sir," the new guest at their table said. "Kaine, I've been wanting to meet you. After all, you're the one who saved my future wife."

Kaine nodded respectfully. "You're welcome, Prince Thane. But I'm no lord, and I got lucky when slaying the monster."

"You're too modest." Thane said, his attention flicking back to the royal families' table. Harkbin and Urith were deep in conversation with King von Stonewall. "I know it's rude of me to ask, especially since you've already helped me, but I was wondering if you could... educate me on a matter of some importance."

"Ask us anything you'd like to know," Eisenbern said, raising his tankard and letting out a loud hiccup.

"Thank you, both of you," Thane said, casting a nervous glance over his shoulder. "I've heard rumors that there is a dangerous sorceress somewhere in your country. Do you think she might be the one who summoned the monster?"

"A sorceress?" Eisenbern burst into laughter. "You Throatians give such fancy names to the Lucidians. They're the only ones with magic, and their Enclave is over a month's ride away from here. Plus, since the end of the war, they've all kept their tails between their legs."

Kaine shook his head at Eisenbern's casual drunkenness in the prince's presence. "Please accept my apologies for our informalities tonight, Prince Thane. We've had a bit too much to drink. The monster is dead and there aren't any more of them, as far as I know. I haven't heard of a sorceress, either. Eisenbern is right that Lucidians would be the only ones who have magic."

"I see." Thane remarked, glancing once more at the table where his family was seated. "There'll be no more monsters for Princess Lydia to worry about then. Thank you again, Kaine. By saving her, you've done us all quite the favor. If you ever venture to our island, I'd be happy to give you the tour."

"That would be great. I've been to your island before, but never beyond White Boar's Landing," Kaine said.

"Of course not," Thane said. "T-those restrictions won't be relevant anymore after the wedding."

The prince winked and returned to his own table. Eisenbern snorted once the prince was out of earshot.

"The Throatian Prince is suddenly a skittish one, ain't he?" Eisenbern said.

"Shut up, Eisenbern." The leader of the Purple

Guard's drunken casualness had reflected poorly on them both as Leilans.

"Come now, you've got to admit he was a little weird. Nobody but Lucidians have magic—besides the Throatians now. It's common sense."

Kaine pushed his most recent empty cup away from his immediate vicinity. "The fact the Throatians gained magic so suddenly changes everything we knew about common sense. Lucidians have always had their power because it's in their bloodlines. The Throatians were isolating themselves for as long as we knew of them, so their source must be something different."

Eisenbern burped. "So, you think Prince Thane wanted to compare notes with a Lucidian? He should know that's controversial. King von Stonewall fought against the Enclave during the war."

"I'm not saying I disagree with you," Kaine said, "but you are aware of the real reason for this wedding, aren't you?"

"The Darian Kingdom needs magic for when the Lucidians decide to collect on their debts and no longer remain neutral."

Kaine scowled. "Their debts?"

"Sorry, wrong word." Eisenbern paused for a few seconds to collect his thoughts. "I mean, after what the Lucidians did to the Yaenia Kingdom, they ran out of wood for their fire—their conquest. But their domination of the Yaenian continent will resume someday. It's not a matter of if, but when. Magic is the only way the Darian Kingdom—and the Leila Kingdom—can resist. By allying with the Throatians, they might protect us, or at least share their secrets, right? Even so, why was Thane asking about a sorceress?"

"Maybe he was trying to be subtle?" Kaine suggested. "As you said, bringing up the Lucidians isn't tactful, but I imagine he's curious to see any other kinds of magic. That's probably all there is to it. Still, it makes me wonder whether the monster I fought in the forest was magical."

Eisenbern chuckled. "Don't overthink it. If the Lucidians were trying to assassinate Lydia, how would they have known she was planning to run away from her wedding? Plus, there's no need to use magic—a simple blade would have obviously worked fine against an unarmed princess. It makes no sense to announce they were trying to kill her, you know?"

Despite his drunkenness, Eisenbern was right. The monster was just a coincidence, and Thane was likely investigating whether it involved magic. Most likely, politics and promises surrounding the event were being discussed behind closed doors—details all beyond what Kaine could know. It was likely that the upper-class nobles were hunting for any tidbits of information they could leverage in their nego-tiations.

"You're right. There's no need to complicate matters further."

Eisenbern raised his tankard. "To simplicity, then."

Surveying his side of the table, Kaine noticed that all his glasses and cups were empty. He raised his outstretched hand, holding an invisible drink. "To simplicity."

The leader of the Purple Guard chugged the rest of his drink. "Well, that's enough for me for tonight. Need to save some room for tomorrow." He patted his belly.

"Same here. We'd best get some rest so we don't look like ghosts at the wedding ceremony tomorrow."

They rose from their chairs, among the last to depart from the dinner. As midnight approached, so too did the time for his meeting with Lydia. He bade Eisenbern goodnight, then made way through the throne room's massive wooden doors, through the empty lobby, and into the cool night air outside, where the light of the day was already long past.

4

THE PRICE OF MAGIC

A shivering chill enveloped his body as Kaine waited for Lydia in the graveyard, as per her request. His cheeks stung from the cold fog that had settled over the castle, moonlight dancing across the damp stone surfaces of the tombstones and crypts. His mouth was dry, but on the whole, he was sober again. Luckily, his tolerance from the years before still seemed intact.

"Kaine," a voice familiar to him echoed through the haze.

"Where are you, Princess Lydia?"

She stepped off a large gravestone from where she'd been sitting and scanned the area for unwanted eyes or ears.

"Over here," she mumbled. "Kaine, there's no

need for such formality when we're alone. It's not that important."

"As you wish," Kaine replied. Why had she chosen a graveyard of all locations to meet?

"Thank you for coming tonight," she whispered. "It means a lot to me." Sometime since the rehearsal dinner, she'd changed into a black dress that seemed far more mature than the others he'd seen her wear previously. Though Kaine hadn't known Lydia for very long, her demeanor seemed different from the other times they'd met, almost as though she was now an entirely different young woman.

"There must be a lot on your mind—the wedding is tomorrow morning. But why meet in this ghastly place?"

Lydia's lips moved, yet no words came out. The princess's fingers still curled around her ring, while her distracted gaze made her seem frantic. After taking a moment, she finally spoke. "You do not understand many things yet, but I feel you're the only person who I can trust with what I'm about to tell you."

"But why me, though?" Kaine asked. "I mean, I'm happy to talk, but am I really the only person you can trust? What about your father or your servants? Compared to them, you barely know me."

"With this, I need someone independent from my

family and subjects," she said. "Everything will make sense soon."

Kaine brushed his hair back with his hands. Lydia's behavior had seemed strange and highly secretive, especially since they'd met with her father. It was clear she was keeping things from him, but what those things were was still a mystery. Was she about to ask him to do something illegal?

It was about time she addressed one of his questions. "Speaking of things making sense, how did you know about the history that Queen Blanche and I share? Nobody should know about that. Who told you?"

The princess drew her lips inward. A moment later, she replied: "It's all connected, and I can explain, but first, I need your word that you'll keep all of this to yourself."

"Yet another secret, then."

Lydia exhaled, absently scratching her ear. "Yes, and I need your help. What I'm going to say—you will not like it, but you can't try to change it. I'll tell you everything. Just promise not to share. Not with anyone, okay?"

"Of course," Kaine promised.

Lydia rolled her neck, attempting to ease the tension. After another moment of silence, she drew in a deep breath. "Months ago, I was curious and found some rare stones belonging to my father. He kept them hidden inside his throne for safekeeping, but I stole them and replaced them with fake ones."

"I assume you're carrying a sense of guilt for stealing them," Kaine concluded. "You can't just return them to your father and apologize?"

Dismissing his suggestion with a shake of her head, she gestured towards a nearby stone bench. As the two of them sat down together, they both looked around to verify that nobody else would overhear their conversation.

"I feel guilty for stealing them, but my feelings don't matter in this," Lydia said. "The stones are magical, and they gave me powers. By disguising them as my rings, I hid them in plain sight. I've always worn a variety of different jewelry and my father's never paid much attention to such insignificant details. He never knew I was using his stones and their magic."

It was common knowledge that only Lucidians had powers. The conduit for their magic was their bodies, and such limitations allowed only simple abilities such as making small amounts of fire, water, and healing wounds. Magical items were unheard of. Assuming Lydia's tale was correct, then everything Kaine knew about Lucidians might have been inaccurate. If the Throatians also learned how to wield magic, then the doorway to supernatural abilities was now open for all other humans, too. Likewise, if magical items also existed, they may have lingered in plain sight all along.

"Incredible," Kaine said. "Your rings must indeed be dangerous. If your father knew, it would worry him."

"No, it's not a matter of guilt or how my father would react. He can't even use their power, so there's no way for him to know the ones I put in his box are fakes."

"So why not just return the stones?"

Lydia stared at her feet. "That's my intention, but it's more complicated than that."

"Did you lose control of the magic?" Kaine asked. "It couldn't be easy to learn. You can fix or atone for any mistakes if that's what happened."

The princess shook her head. "Just touching the stones lets me unlock their powers as naturally as breathing. It was almost too easy. The problem is that I've done some terrible things and learned so much about the world that I'm not supposed to know."

"For instance?"

She gulped. "Tonight, at the rehearsal dinner, I found out I am going to die when my wedding is over."

Kaine blinked, rubbing his forehead in disbelief. Even with magic, could she foresee a fixed future, or merely a possibility?

"How can you know for certain that it will happen?"

Tears, casting the glint of the moonlight, traced paths down Lydia's otherwise impassive face. She held her silence for another moment and then explained. "Each stone has a special magic. One of my rings allows me to copy someone else's memories into my mind as if they were my own. It's how I knew so much about you. I've seen your entire past —everything you remember. I'm so sorry that I didn't respect your privacy, but I was curious about you. It was this same power that told me I'm going to die. Thane's, Harkbin's, and Urith's minds all have it."

"Don't worry about me. I'm not mad at you," Kaine assured her, forcing a half-smile. Truthfully, her actions did unsettle him, yet more pressing issues demanded his attention at the moment. "Your reading of my memories is insignificant compared to what you've just revealed. How does one read someone's future memory? Do your father's stones let you see the future too?"

"It's not as simple as that. Memories are inherently from the past," Lydia said. "Reading someone's past is my only useful power. I don't quite understand how to use the other stones yet. They give me bad feelings. My two handmaidens died because I didn't know how to use the other stones properly."

It tempted Kaine to ask whether the monster somehow ate them both, but that didn't feel relevant at the moment. The implications of the magic at her disposal were more urgent. "But I still don't understand how you can know the future by reading somebody else's memory."

"I used the ring during the dancing earlier because I wanted to learn more about my future husband. In his memories, I saw several meetings from before the Asche family left their homeland. After we're married, they are planning to sacrifice me to their god. My blood is valuable to them."

Rising from the bench, Kaine declared, "This is horrendous! We must cancel the wedding immediately and remove the Throatians from the kingdom!"

Lydia shook her head. "No, we can't take action. I must follow through with this. With everything." She stood up next to him. "I've read my father's memories and seen his secret council meetings. My father fears the Throatians. Their magic is real—it comes from their god. Their sacrifices trade human lives for magic. They—"

"It isn't right," Kaine interrupted. "Why should you have to die so they can have their magic? Your father would never go through with the wedding if he knew what they were planning. Why can't you say anything?"

"He'd go to war with them if he knew their intentions," Lydia said. "We would lose it, and many would die. I've seen the Throatian magic in their memories. Before they sailed here for the wedding, they killed a bunch of prisoners with lightning by asking their god. The magic came from the sky, not from a person."

Mass murder from a god couldn't be possible, but Throatians believing in the power of a sacrifice was a different issue. "There has to be some way around this. We can't let them sacrifice you. Perhaps the lightning you saw was but a coincidence?"

"It's real. There's no escaping this," Lydia said. "If I disappear before the wedding, my father will lose the alliance. If I disappear during or after the wedding, it's the same result. I'm the price to ensure the Darian Kingdom's safety."

"How do you know they won't just betray your father, anyway? Based on what you've revealed, they hardly seem trustworthy."

"It was in the Throatians' meetings. They plan to leave the Darian Kingdom alone after the wedding. I'm worth a lot of magic to them once they bring me home. They need it. That's what they believe."

Kaine stared up at the sky through some gaps in the fog and took a deep breath. Thousands of stars were burning somewhere off in the distance, scattered so far away within the galaxy's darkness. Among them all, was there also a maleficent foreign god demanding that Lydia kill herself by marrying Prince Thane? Were the Throatians so greedy that they'd go to such lengths to betray the von Stonewall family? It wasn't right, even if he was only halfway correct.

Kaine sighed. "I don't want you to die. It isn't fair. There has to be some other way for them to get their magic."

"Human lives are the sole means," Lydia stated. "I don't understand why, but I am apparently worth several of them. If not me, then the Throatians will take many, many others in my place."

Kaine racked his mind for an idea. Her father feared the Throatians because of their magic, but they might only have their power because of the sacrifices. If there were a way to stop their god from supplying the magic, then Lydia wouldn't have to die.

"What do we know about their god? Have you seen it in their memories?"

"They've only witnessed magic when their god provides it," Lydia said. "None of the Asche family has actually seen their god in a physical form, but it somehow passed instructions down through Harkbin and his late father. So, the sacrifices must have been happening for a long time already. You're looking for a loophole in their plan, aren't you?"

"Yes, if we gather enough details, we can find a way to—"

"There isn't a way that works, even knowing everything there is to know of it," Lydia said. "I carry all their memories inside me. They aren't the sort of people who will negotiate. They believe what they're doing is right. And I need to protect Kira too."

She had a point. Kaine hadn't even considered that Lydia's younger sister might also be in danger, and it would soon be his job to protect her. "They might be after Princess Kira?"

"She's only in danger if I don't go," Lydia said. "My sacrifice should keep them from needing royal blood for a long time. I've already decided to go through with it, but I need your help with some things before I do."

"No, you can't!" Kaine exclaimed. "How could you accept it?"

"At first, I didn't want to be the sacrifice, either, but this is the only resolution that doesn't lead to other people suffering. And even if we found a way for me to somehow live through this wedding, I don't want to marry someone who kills others in the name of their religion."

"I understand."

With one arm, she wiped away her tears and continued. "When you saved me in the forest, I was running away from the wedding because I feared everything that might come with it. Now that I know the reality is far worse, I can't justify living through it either way. I refuse to be part of a family that kills for the sake of magic."

"That's it," Kaine said. "The Asche family wants you dead. If we can take them by surprise, then maybe we can kill them before they can use their magic."

"No, that isn't what I needed your help with," Lydia said. "We could murder the royal family, yes. Still, they have a political opponent at home who wants to seize the Throatian throne. He is someone even more devout to their evil religion. Killing the Asche family will allow that person in their homeland to seize control. War would still make its way to the Darian Kingdom."

They lapsed into silence, both lost in their thoughts amidst the eerie quiet of the graveyard.

"Kaine, I know the pain that's in your heart. I know you regret leaving the Leila Kingdom behind and that you're scared to join us and make the same mistake again."

"I don't know."

"You can't let your anxiety dominate you," Lydia said. "Stop isolating yourself from those you love because you're afraid they'll judge you. You saw what happened with your parents. There wasn't a way for you to know back then, but now you do. Life continues without you and people grow older. Hiding yourself away because of your darkest feelings is the same as taking it all for granted."

She was right, but it wasn't her privilege to know. It was as if she'd thrown all his greatest fears, pains, and experiences on the ground in front of them and was nitpicking them all. Kaine had said it was okay, but now he realized it wasn't.

"Stop it. Please." His skin tingled with each word. "I don't want to talk about it."

She placed her delicate, bejeweled hand on his shoulder. "I'm sorry about that. I don't mean to preach. It's just that I want you to find happiness with my family once I'm gone, Kaine. They'll accept you for who you are. You've lost too much already, and while my family is no replacement for that, they'll help fill some of the void. In turn, you can fill in some of the emptiness I'll leave behind."

Tears traced their path down his cheeks. The princess he had encountered in the forest and the young woman he was talking to now seemed like two completely different people. Regardless, she was right.

"Black sands of Tornaa. I hate this so much." Kaine wiped his eyes. "I'll do everything I can to stop running, but what can I do for you? Are you certain we can't somehow save you from the Throatians?"

"We're stuck. I'm going through with the sacrifice, but I need to make sure that my father doesn't go to battle with the Throatian Kingdom when I die. I have two tasks for you."

She walked over to a nearby gravestone, reached behind its base, and then held out a sealed envelope for him. "This is a letter I wrote. You need to pretend to find it in Prince Xander's chambers. Don't open or reveal the letter to anyone until after the wedding. Not until after I've sailed away from Starlight Beach with the Throatians."

Kaine took the envelope from her trembling hands. The pouch was light purple and sealed in wax depicting her initials: LVS. The packet was light-weight, so the letter inside must have been short or written in a small script.

"Understood. I promise not to unseal it. But, may I inquire about its contents?"

"It's a letter from me that will prevent my father from engaging the Throatians in war."

"I don't understand, but I trust you know what you're doing."

"I do."

Kaine pocketed the envelope. "So, what's the second task?"

"I want you to help me return my father's magical stones to the throne, so they'll remain with him after I'm gone," Lydia said. "I don't know everything about them, but I know they would be dangerous in the hands of the wrong people. Opening the secret compartment inside the throne takes a few minutes. Can you be my lookout?"

"Understood," Kaine said. "Then we should try sneaking into the throne room now. It's late, and everyone is probably asleep."

"I appreciate your assistance," Lydia said. "Fixing these wrongs is my Everlasting Wish. I won't be able to say it during the wedding ceremony, but this is my truth."

KAINE AND LYDIA STEALTHILY ENTERED THE DIMLY lit, deserted throne room. The party tables, chairs, and other decorations from the extravagant rehearsal dinner remained set up for the next morning's wedding. Light from a lone candle hanging on the rear wall provided just enough illumination for them to ascertain that they were alone. Kaine held his breath, waiting in the doorway as Lydia tiptoed down the aisle, where the ceremony would happen in a matter of hours.

"This won't take long," she whispered. "Cough if you hear anyone coming and I'll hide behind the drapery."

"And what if I'm caught?"

"Pretend that you forgot your coin purse at your chair during the rehearsal dinner. Don't worry—this will only take a minute."

As the princess moved forward, a gust of icy wind swept through the windows, brushing against Kaine's face and causing him to flinch, the stubble on his face prickling. He waited patiently, his vision straining as Lydia tinkered with the base of the throne across the room, out of his sight. There was a resounding click, a thud, and then she gasped.

"They're gone," she said. "Someone already removed the fake stones from the secret chamber."

"What?" Kaine whispered back.

"Just a moment."

Another click echoed from the distant side as Lydia closed the secret compartment. Next, her shoes echoed across the floor as she returned to him.

"We must leave swiftly," she murmured.

They stepped outside into the courtyard, and the moon's position revealed it was well past midnight already.

"Everything's as it should be now." Lydia's voice weakened as she stared at the ground for a moment. "Yes, I'm pretty sure my father is the one who removed the fake stones. It must have been a while ago."

"What do you mean by pretty sure?" Kaine

pressed. "This seems really important. Who else knows they're hidden here?"

"Only the council members, but they know not to touch them. The Throatians are after the stones too, but they're looking in all the wrong places—I saw it in their memories. They sent their guards out into the city's churches and into my father's chambers. They won't find them, nor have they suspected the stones' location."

Kaine tightened his folded arms close to his chest. "And what if someone else did? This seems too risky to not investigate."

"If someone else stole them, then they'll have the counterfeits," Lydia pointed out. "It's unlikely they'd return to the same spot to check for whether real ones replaced the decoys. Plus, my father would have sent the guards to investigate if he thought somebody stole them."

He gave an approving nod. "Perhaps so—I noticed you're often fiddling with your rings. If he recognized the stones on your fingers were his, then he already knew you had them."

Lydia sighed. "Your conjecture is likely the truth. It's unlikely for anyone but my father or the council members to know about the secret compartment. I thought he was none the wiser about me taking them."

"I'm confident he'll forgive you," Kaine said. "But

you should still confirm whether he's the one who removed the fakes."

He carefully scrutinized their surroundings, making sure they were still alone. It would be better if they returned to the graveyard or somewhere more private before anyone else saw them. "We should head back."

Silently, they retraced their steps back toward the graveyard. A few minutes went by before Lydia broke the quietness. "Everything should be okay now. I've returned the stones and learned my lesson about carelessly using their magic. If you're still worried about it, you can check the secret compartment sometime once the wedding is over and we're gone. Just add a light pressure near the base of the chair's rear and you'll find it. Either way, what's done is done."

"Okay."

As they neared the entrance archway next to the initial tombstones, Kaine blurted, "I still don't want you to die. There's truly nothing we can do to prevent this?"

"I've lived many years as a princess here in the capital," Lydia said, her voice shaking. "It's a better life than most other girls get. It's my destiny to be sacrificed; nobody should see it as tragic. Why shouldn't I close the book of my existence while everything is still ahead? I'll be preventing war and other people's suffering at the same time."

They found themselves back at the cluster of graves where they'd previously conversed and sat down again in the same spot.

"It shouldn't have to be you," Kaine said, trying to keep his voice down. "You're a good person."

"Goodness is subjective—I've done some serious things with my father's stones. Along the way, I've betrayed so many people's privacy and trust."

"Innocent or not, there has to be something we can do about the Throatians," Kaine said. "We just need more time to think."

"I probably deserve this," Lydia replied. "If I had just left those stones well enough alone, I wouldn't have learned my fate beforehand. Tomorrow, I would be nervous like any other girl, excited about my life ahead. Still, I'm glad I could see the truth and set things right before I go."

Kaine frowned. "You don't deserve this at all; your foresight doesn't alter that fact."

The princess sighed. "Maybe that's so. But who are we to conclude it? We aren't gods and goddesses." She stood from the bench. "I'm sorry, I forgot that I have something for you."

She moved behind the gravestone, where she'd previously concealed her letter and reached behind it again. This time, she produced a small bottle of wine for him. "This is for you. I never properly thanked you for saving me from the monster. Please consume it tonight to wish me good luck for tomorrow. Don't share it with anybody. It's quite rare, and I only want you to enjoy it."

Kaine took the gift from her trembling hands. "Okay, I will drink it in your honor. It's not poisoned, right?" He tried to ease the tension by winking, but she didn't seem to notice. Lydia seemed oddly content with her fate, almost unbelievably so. She wasn't showing it, but Kaine suspected she'd been hiding her greater fears from him.

"Don't be silly, Kaine."

She leaned forward and gave him a hug and a kiss on the cheek. "Your help this evening means so much to me. You're the only person who can know the truth. The letter I gave you will handle the rest. I look forward to seeing you tomorrow, Kaine. Goodnight."

5

THE GOD STONES

Back in his newly assigned chamber, Kaine tossed a few logs into the fireplace. Despite the night being three-quarters gone, his mind was still wide awake. With his arms clasped behind his back, he paced beside the growing flames. Though the warmth was comforting, his thoughts sent chills down his spine. He strode over to the nearby table and poured himself a modest amount of the gift Lydia had given him. Wine usually sharpened his thoughts, lending them clarity and creativity, and the princess's wine had a sweet taste. He took a large gulp and continued pacing.

There was no conceivable way to prevent the wedding without instigating a war, was there? In a full-on fight against the Throatian Kingdom, the Darian Kingdom would lose because they had no magic. The Throatians just wanted Lydia so they could sacrifice her, so was there a way to trick them into thinking they'd succeeded while saving Lydia? He took another sip.

It seemed unachievable. The Asche royal family would presumably kill her after bringing her back to their homeland. There was no way they would make the sacrifice while she was still on Darian soil. Lydia was right; she was stuck. There had to be some way to keep her alive and keep the Darian Kingdom's relationship with the Throatian Kingdom intact.

Kaine's fingers traced the edges of the envelope that Lydia had given him as he recalled her words: "A letter from me that will prevent my father from engaging the Throatians in war."

The princess had been clear she did not want him to open the letter until after the wedding, but why? What could be inside that he should not know until later? Undoubtedly, the contents of her letter were worth knowing beforehand.

He placed the wine goblet on the adjacent table and examined the envelope closer. She should have at least shared all the information with him before making him promise not to open it. Lydia had planned everything out but did not bother to ask his opinion on anything before recruiting him to carry out her plans. He knew he was breaking his promise to her, but he needed all the information available to figure out something. He tiptoed over to his bedroom door and locked it.

He drew his pocketknife from his leather pouch, wrapping the hilt in one of his shirts. Holding the knife over the flames, he let the blade burn and whiten. Then he slid it underneath the letter's wax seal and jiggled it back and forth. The seal split, yet Lydia's signature on the surface remained intact. He'd be able to reseal it again later.

He slid the thin sheet of paper from the purple envelope. With his hands trembling from both nerves and alcohol, he read what Lydia meant for him to not see until tomorrow:

Father,

It hurts me to say this, but I've done something terrible. I've betrayed the entire kingdom. By the time you read this, I will already be in the Throatian Kingdom with my new husband. Nobody knew I was pregnant before the wedding; that's been my secret and why I ran away from the castle. I won't say who the father is, but when the Asche family finds out I am with child, I will not remain under their grace. I am so ashamed of what I've done. Please do not seek revenge on the Throatian Kingdom if they punish me. I deserve whatever comes my way. Please do not go to war with the Throatians. This is my sincere Everlasting Wish.

I will ask the Throatians to spread rumors that I died of a fever so that no shame will come upon the von Stonewall family name. I'm sorry it ended like this.

Words cannot express how much pain and guilt I feel now. Please tell Xander and Kira that I love them. And thank you for everything you've done for me, father. For my entire life, I've tried my best to do good as you taught me, but this one mistake will cost me everything.

Always,
LVS

"DID SHE FABRICATE THIS LIE TO PREVENT HER FATHER from attacking the Throatians?" Kaine murmured in a hushed tone.

He fought the urge to crumple the paper and instead clutched his almost-empty wine bottle, continuing to drink. As he paced the room, letter in one hand, bottle in the other, he read the princess's words repeatedly until her gift to him was empty. Lydia was already lining up to sacrifice herself to protect her kingdom; it was unfair she should tarnish her relationship with her father too. Writing lies about herself and ruining her reputation to save everyone… it wasn't right.

He leaned back in his chair and cast a sidelong glance out the window to confirm that the sun hadn't yet risen.

"I can't let her go through with this—neither with the sacrifice nor the lies," Kaine muttered to himself. Meanwhile, his face burned as he considered whether there was any realistic way of saving her.

He couldn't stand by as Lydia compromised her dignity with a deception that would lead her father into believing she was pregnant. He tossed the letter into the fireplace and watched it burn. After the paper disintegrated to ash, he grabbed the envelope and burned it too. Kaine had saved Lydia's honor, but the problem of how to save her life remained.

"What can I do?" he wondered aloud again. He squatted next to the fireplace and watched the flames, praying that an idea would come. There was something obvious he was missing.

Kaine was unable to discern what impelled him to have such a deep concern for Lydia. Saving the princess was the right thing to do, but he couldn't fathom why he felt so compelled to solve the insurmountable problems she faced. With Ether von Stonewall having recruited Kaine into his house, a clear duty to protect her now rested on his shoulders. But beyond those obligations, something else was there—Lydia was kind and genuinely cared about her kingdom and its people. If she ever became queen of the Darian Kingdom, she'd do right by it. Saving her would have more effects on the future than Kaine could ever know.

Plus, something about her reading his mind had established a connection between the two of them. Yes—by Lydia learning about his entire past and diagnosing a hidden darkness, a greater reason formed. She'd helped him realize the source of a shadow that had plagued his subconscious self for years. Defeating it opened a path to enlightenment, and he couldn't have understood any of it without her. In a way, she had saved him. It was only right that he repay her.

"I can't leave this unfinished," he muttered to the empty room. Rescuing her from the monster was pointless, if it only meant condemning her to the Throatians.

Kaine stretched out on the floor next to the fire, attempting to calm his nerves. The room was spinning from the wine. With just a bit of rest, surely an idea would come. Something would arrive, and he would figure out how to save her and prevent a war. There had to be some way of stopping the Throatians. His drunkenness would bring him creativity and clarity—it had to. He closed his eyes and continued pondering.

"SIR KHALIA!" CALLED A SERVANT THROUGH HIS chamber door. "Are you ill?"

Kaine opened his eyes, the world tilting sideways as sunlight pierced his room, blinding him. Out of the corner of his vision, he could see a wooden wall —no, those were floorboards. He had fallen asleep on the floor near the fireplace, which was now flameless and filled with ash. Kaine blinked as he stood, his whole body tense and achy from his uncomfortable position on the floor. Next to where he had slept, there was vomit. Cursing himself for overindulging once again, he slowly rose and dusted himself off.

"Sir Khalia?" the voice repeated.

"Yes, I was sick," Kaine replied, opening his door to greet the servant who had brought him breakfast.

"I brought you a plate from the wedding," the attendant said. "Roasted chicken with mashed potatoes and—"

"The wedding! It's over?" Kaine exclaimed. "What time is it?"

The servant nodded. "It's just after midday, sir. And unfortunately, yes, you've missed the wedding. A few servants tried to wake you earlier this morning, but we couldn't get through your snores and groans. My apologies, Sir Khalia. It ended about an hour ago, but I brought you some brunch."

"Where's the princess now?" Kaine asked. "Please tell me. I need to talk with her."

"I don't know precisely, but she is probably on her way to Starlight Beach with the Throatian royalty by now. Their ships will depart from there."

"What about the king?" Kaine demanded. "I need to find him."

"The king is currently escorting the Throatian family."

"Black sand!" Kaine bellowed, shutting the door in the servant's face.

Still dressed in his clothes from the night before, it took all of ten minutes to rush down to the stables, sword at his waist. He seized the first horse he could and galloped as fast as possible through Last Hope's roads. He could not afford to waste any time. Though Kaine lacked a plan, he was determined to rescue the princess. Reaching the main gate, he yelled at the guard to open it. "Please hurry!"

"Hey, Boring Knight," a voice echoed from behind him. "What's the hurry?"

Kaine looked around and saw Eisenbern standing by the gate. He seemed to have just finished eating his lunch, as various crumbs rested entangled within his beard.

"Come with me," Kaine yelled back. "The princess is in danger."

Eisenbern froze, then patted his hip to confirm that his sword was with him. "Let's go. You can tell me about it on the way. You, there!" He pointed at a guard. "Gather me forty men and join us down the road toward Starlight Beach."

Eisenbern borrowed a horse from the guard. As the security gate lowered, the two men sped down the trail, the capital city swiftly receding into the distance behind them.

"What's going on?" Eisenbern asked as they sped down the dirt pathway. "Why did you miss the wedding?"

Kaine sighed. "Long story short, I drank too much. But I think Princess Lydia is in danger from the Throatians. I'm certain they want to kill her."

"That makes no sense! They wouldn't kill their prince's new wife!"

"I'm a hundred percent sure of it," Kaine said. "There might be nothing else we can do but apprehend the Throatian royalty and hope they can't overpower us with their magic."

"What you're talking about is treason if you're wrong, you know," Eisenbern warned. "As Leilans, we're allied with the Darians—that includes the Throatians now, too. How did you learn of this? They have shown no hostility or hinted toward wanting to harm the princess. They married their son to her after all!"

"Remember how the king and queen insisted last night on blessing their chickens before killing them? Their magic derives from sacrificing something alive to their god. Since Lydia is a princess, her life might be worth more, it seems."

"Well, I don't know where you're getting all these ideas from, but it can't hurt to provide more escorts," Eisenbern said.

"Thank you for trusting me," Kaine said. "Look at it this way: why stop at chickens when you can fabricate a marriage to kidnap a princess? We must hurry!"

THE TWO OF THEM GALLOPED ALONG THE DIRT ROADS, cutting through grassy fields for nearly an hour, but there was no sign of King Ether von Stonewall's carriage. Kaine's head pounded from his hangover, and he struggled to breathe. Sweat dripped down his forehead, stinging his tired eyes. The morning sunlight was ruthless, and the road they raced down offered no shade for comfort until they reached the forest where Kaine had slain the monster. They hoped to catch up soon.

"Look!" Eisenbern yelled, pointing. "The king is over there. Is he okay?"

Further down the road, a man in red clothes was curled over with his forehead touching the ground. He was shaking, so at least he was still alive. Kaine did not need to get closer to recognize him. The two of them approached and dismounted their horses.

"My king!" Kaine called out as King Ether looked up at them.

"Lydia," he cried out. "She's gone."

Kaine fell to his knees. "She can't be."

Eisenbern gripped the king under his arm to help him up. "Can you stand? Whose blood is this? Were you hurt?"

Kaine stared at the king's bloodstained clothes, but he already knew the answer—the blood wasn't Ether's.

"Lydia," her father stammered. "They stabbed her and left with her body. She's dead."

"No. What you saw was wrong," Kaine said, hands shaking in disbelief. It had to be. He took a deep breath. Knees slightly jerking, he stood and assisted Eisenbern in lifting the king.

"I understand," Eisenbern said, taking charge of the situation. "We have reinforcements on the way. I'll head back and meet them halfway. We'll send a bird toward Starlight Beach. Kaine will stay here and take care of you, okay?"

The king nodded, unable or unwilling to say anything else.

"Kaine, you were right about the Throatians after all," Eisenbern admitted. "Lydia's gone, but this isn't over. I don't know what kind of religion the Throatians are following, but today isn't the end."

He looked at Eisenbern and tried to say it was too late and that nothing else mattered, but his mouth failed to open. His lips could barely move, and his tongue was numb. His tightened throat dominated all his sensations. This was all his fault.

Eisenbern slapped Kaine's shoulder. "Pull yourself together, Kaine Khalia! Do you hear me? Take care of your king. Get him farther up the road to some shade so he doesn't succumb to heatstroke. I'm going to bring more soldiers."

The Leila Kingdom's knight quickly shifted his

horse around and rode off into the distance. He left no time for Kaine to discuss or debate the decision.

Kaine turned aside and vomited. The reality was too stark for him to accept. The king was also in shock, and Kaine couldn't imagine how much heavier Ether von Stonewall's pain was than his own. Kaine had known Lydia for less than a week. The king had lost his daughter.

"It's going to be okay. I don't know how or when, but it will be."

The king, still staring off into the air, shook his head. "My heart."

Kaine stammered to find words. The shock jumbled his lips for what felt like minutes before he could say anything at all.

"My first baby girl," the king sobbed. "My rose! They murdered her on her wedding day. A lone knight in crimson armor was waiting for us here and stopped our carriage. Harkbin got out, and I heard them arguing for a while in their Throatian language. Prince Thane gave the crimson knight a satchel and then they called everyone out of the carriage."

"A satchel?" Kaine asked. "Was there gold inside it?"

"I don't know, and it doesn't matter," Ether said. "I tried to get them to take me instead, but they said they only wanted Lydia. The Throatian escorts put her in the middle of their circle, then the Asche family yelled their sacrificial blessings as they got closer and…"

He choked on his own words as he struggled to explain.

"And—and then what?" Kaine urged. It was too late to make a difference, but he wanted to know.

The king nodded, still sniffling. "They made her kneel in the dirt. Then Prince Thane stabbed her in the stomach, over and over, while saying his cursed foreign words. I'll never be able to forgive them, Kaine. Lydia's screams were the most pain I've ever felt. Watching my child die like that—what they did to her—it's pure evil."

"She can't be…" Kaine let out, still in disbelief. Why had the plan changed? Why had they killed Lydia so soon? Nothing made sense. "Can we make it to Starlight Beach before they board their ships?"

Kaine's words seemed to rally his king. Ether von Stonewall hauled himself off the ground and helped Kaine to his feet.

"I hope so," Ether said as they walked together toward the trees. "None of it makes sense. Why did they have to murder my daughter? Why her and not me?"

"It's because Lydia is special," Kaine explained. "When they kill people, their god supposedly gives them magic in return. Being a princess must have made her more valuable to trade."

Ether von Stonewall's face went blank. "But the blood of a king should be worth more than a princess. They should have killed me instead. Lydia was just nineteen years old. Why did they have to take her too after doing all this?"

He was right—blood must have been the reason. Lydia had the ability to use the king's magical stones, even though the king himself could not. But how could the Throatians have known that?

"My king," Kaine said. "Lydia shared a secret with me after I saved her from the monster earlier. She could use your magical stones. Power over the stones might relate to the blood of her mother. You should test Xander and Kira to see whether they can use the magic. I don't know how the Throatians would have known, but everything seems connected."

The king grabbed Kaine's shoulders. "Lydia knew about the God Stones? Have you told anyone else?"

"No, nobody else knows."

"Good," Ether said, releasing him. "Do not mention them to anyone. I was unaware that Lydia even knew about them, let alone used them. Tell me more… what did my daughter tell you? What did she know? The God Stones are my most closely guarded secret."

Kaine couldn't tell him that Lydia knew she was going to die. The king would never forgive him if he learned Kaine had known Lydia's fate beforehand.

"She told me she had used a stone once before," Kaine lied. "It let her see herself from someone else's perspective. She got scared and put it away again."

"I see. So, she touched the Memories Stone then. She must have used the Transformation Stone too—that explains the monster you fought in the forest. I can't believe I didn't make the connection. Did she tell you anything else?"

"No, sir."

He remembered that during their encounter in the forest, Lydia's first words had been an apology. Now, the scattered puzzle pieces were aligning in his mind, casting an eerie clarity on the situation. It was Lydia, in her innocence and curiosity, who had created the monster, the ferocious beast he had so fiercely battled. She had fled Last Hope with two handmaidens and lost them both because she had touched a God Stone and couldn't control its magic. The unforeseen consequences of her actions, the havoc it wreaked, and the lives it claimed must have weighed heavily upon her. Such guilt had likely influenced all her subsequent decisions.

"Very few people know about my possession of the God Stones, and I doubt anyone could've foreseen Lydia's ability to use them," Ether von

Stonewall said. "We have to protect them more than anything else we have. They are too dangerous."

"What are the God Stones exactly? Where do they come from?" Kaine asked. "How many are there?"

"I'm sorry, Sir Khalia. I trust you, but all I can say is someone gave them to me during the war, and we have to look after them above all else. The world would be in great danger if they ever fell into the wrong hands!"

"Could we use them against the Throatians, though, if we found someone who could control them?"

"We dare not," the king said. "Even if my other children could harness the stones, they are too perilous to be brought to public knowledge. If the world learned that we possessed four God Stones, every nation would conspire to seize them. I trust only my council members with this information—and now you. Do not disclose the existence of the God Stones to anyone. Never even imply that we have a secret that is this important. Is that clear?"

"As clear as your crystal throne, sir." Kaine hesitated. "There's something else. Someone removed the fake stones from your throne before Lydia put the real ones back. She told me. Was it you?"

"No," Ether growled. "It must have been the Throatians. I can't believe they discovered the compartment. Thank Asura that Lydia…" His voice faltered for a moment. "She saved us. It's pure luck, but so long as the stones remain there, Harkbin, Urith, and Thane won't get everything they wanted."

"I understand," Kaine said. "So, what can we do next?"

"We will avenge her, somehow," the king said, nodding his head. "I promise that as soon as the soldiers arrive, we will hunt them down and do what we must. They may have magic, but a sword will pierce them the same as any other man. The Throatians will pay the price for their treachery. Where are those guards that Eisenbern sent?" As he spoke, a vein in Ether's temple throbbed visibly, and his face darkened.

"They'll be here soon," Kaine promised. "I trust Eisenbern. He won't fail us."

Everything was moving in the direction Lydia had wanted to prevent, but now that she was gone, Kaine couldn't help but agree with the king's reaction. The Throatians hadn't even given Ether the courtesy of bringing Lydia back to their island before murdering her. Forcing Lydia's father to witness their sacrifice introduced an entirely new level of cruelty to the situation. It also made Lydia's previous letter redundant—even if Kaine hadn't already drunkenly burned it. He couldn't help but ponder what Lydia would have wished for him to do next, now that everything had gone so tragically awry.

"Everything is going to hinge on him," the king said. "Without troops, we lose the battle before it begins."

6

THE END OF INNOCENCE

Eisenbern led forty armored soldiers on horseback to where Kaine and their king were waiting. They brought extra horses for the king and Kaine, helped them mount, then continued their way toward Starlight Beach. Kaine rode with Eisenbern and Ether at the head of the troops.

"Why isn't General Kern with us?" Ether von Stonewall asked.

"He's dead," Eisenbern declared. "After the ceremony, he returned to his chambers to change clothes. Someone smashed his head in with a war hammer there. A servant told a guard, who reported it to me."

The king swore. "And next in line is…" He took a

moment to think. "I'm sorry. I can't think straight right now. Did anyone volunteer to lead?"

"I rallied whoever I could find as quickly as I could," Eisenbern said. "As far as I know, none of your highest ranks are here. News is spreading in Last Hope about this and when they get the word, more troops will come."

"For now, you're leading the men you brought with you," Ether said. "Queen Blanche placed her trust in you, and her judgment has my trust."

"Our kingdoms are sisters," Eisenbern said. "Doing so honors both."

"That's the spirit we need right now," Ether said.

They journeyed further along the road for another ten minutes, but the path and grassy plains surrounding them were bare of anyone else.

"They likely still have Lydia's body," Kaine announced, now suited in silver armor the soldiers had brought for him. "Do you think we can catch them before they leave the ports of Starlight Beach?"

Before Eisenbern could reply, he inhaled dust from the road, now clouded from hoofbeats, and coughed several times. After clearing his throat and spitting some phlegm off to the side of the road, he answered. "Their carriage can only move so fast. If we keep up this pace, we'll get them by surprise. It's unlikely they know Kaine figured out their intentions."

More clouds of dirt rose from where the horses galloped. Eisenbern was right; their pace was quick and there was plenty of time to catch the Throatians before Starlight Beach. The problem was that nobody knew what kind of magical abilities their enemies would have from sacrificing Princess Lydia.

"They'll regret everything they did to my daughter," Ether vowed. "Thank you both... for assisting me."

"I'm not the one to thank," Eisenbern said. "It's because of Kaine that we're here. If not for him, we'd —"

Kaine ignored the compliment. It was nice he was giving him so much credit, but in the end, it was still his fault he hadn't acted sooner. Lydia was dead. Guilt continued eating away at him, and he avoided speaking to anyone else for the rest of the day.

UNDER THE STARS, THE TROOPS AND HORSES RESTED for the night and just before sunrise the next morning, they resumed the pursuit. Eisenbern insisted they would reach the Throatians before midday; they'd reached the forest where the trees surrounding them were thick, but the shaded road was easy to follow. Deeper into the forest, they stumbled upon the royal carriage, deserted in the middle of the road.

Ether removed himself from his horse, then drew his blade. "Let's investigate. Maybe bandits got them?"

Kaine and Eisenbern dismounted as well, swords also drawn. Holding his breath, Kaine quietly walked over to the horseless vehicle. There were no signs of a struggle. Birds sang and chirped peacefully in the nearby trees, and it was likely the Throatians had intentionally left the carriage behind. They must have realized they were being followed and increased their pace.

With a finger to his lips, Eisenbern gestured with his free hand for Kaine to open the carriage door so he could peer inside. Hands sweating, Kaine gripped the golden handle and pulled it. As the heavy wooden door squeaked open, Eisenbern lunged forward, sword first.

"Nothing inside," he said. "Looks like they took the horses and ran."

As Ether continued observing them, Kaine let the door go and wiped his hands on a small piece of his shirt peeking out from underneath his armor. "I wonder whether they stayed on the road. If they knew we were following them, they might have diverted. They might be traveling parallel to it now."

"I doubt they know these lands well enough to detour very far. They're probably less than a mile off the path, but still heading south."

The king sheathed his blade and then mounted his horse. "I'm not sure I agree," he declared from his mount. "The road through this forest is the fastest way to get to Starlight Beach. Time is of the essence for them, and I doubt they'd waste time hiding. Plus, Merdel told me he originally brought them through the eastern path, not through here. They won't know this forest well. Nevertheless, I suppose none of that matters. They're cowards for killing my daughter in cold blood, but they're smart enough to realize that once they make it to their boats, they'll have the advantage of the sea. The Darian Fleet is at Wargonne right now—we only have civilian ships and a few patrols where we're going."

"That could become a problem later. We should rest here for now and scout for a moment. The horses are tired," Eisenbern said. "Kaine and I can look around on foot and determine whether they stayed on the road."

He walked over to where the carriage stood and quietly peered into the nearby trees. Clouds had formed overhead and rain began falling from the skies, dripping onto him from the branches above. So long as the weather remained mild, it wouldn't affect their travels, but they would need to assume the worst.

"I'm going to scout for tracks," Eisenbern said, then added, "If the rain picks up, it'll be harder to figure out where they went. Kaine, can you check the other side?"

"Understood."

Kaine was rusty at tracking animals or people, but if there were any traces of footprints, dropped belongings, or broken branches, he would find them. He walked around the outskirts into the brushes and surrounding trees, scanning for hints. The rain soon picked up, producing an enchanting symphony of rain within the forest. His armor became drenched and chilled, but the sounds of the raindrops hitting it somehow reminded him of his time at sea. Nature's calmness was short-lived, however. Less than a minute later, Eisenbern yelled for Kaine to return to the road.

"King von Stonewall, how many horses were in the Throatians' possession when you departed Last Hope?" Eisenbern asked. His face was pale and covered in what looked like rain, but could have been sweat.

"Eight horses," Ether replied. "Four moving the carriage and four escorts. Why?"

"You're going to want to see this. Follow me."

He led the two of them away from the road. They

walked until they reached a small clearing among the trees. All eight of the Throatians' horses lay dead on the ground, their bodies lined up in a circle. A large pool of blood, frothing from the rain, sat in the middle of the arranged corpses. As Kaine approached the man-made basin, his mouth remained open in awe. Finally, right in front of the sacrificial pit, he picked up a metal tankard they'd left behind. Dried blood covered both the inside and outside of the container.

"How in the black sands of Tornaa did they do this?" Kaine blurted. Throwing the tankard into the basin, he accidentally splashed himself with blood. Cursing again, he made his way over to the nearest corpse and squatted down next to it. His fingers carefully stroked the dead horse's face, damp and cold. Buried within the red-stained fur on its neck was a large slit from where the Throatians had drained the blood. It was too cruel.

"It's the same ritual we saw with the chickens at the rehearsal dinner," he said. "This time, instead of using a bowl for the blood sacrifice, they dug a basin in the ground."

Eisenbern was off on his own, examining another corpse and shaking his head. "They cut the horse's leg tendons first so they couldn't run away. Maybe they knocked it unconscious first. I don't know. Never have I seen the relationship between man and horse violated so deeply. Eight perfectly fine and healthy horses, all gutted."

"They'll pay for their cruelty," declared the king. His face was expressionless, but his hands, hidden below his waist, were tensed into fists. "I should have never allied with them. No magic is worth this price."

"I don't understand why they'd kill their horses though," Eisenbern said. "The Throatians needed them for speed. If they're traveling on foot now, what was the point? They'll only move slower going forward. We can catch them."

"They sacrificed them for magic," Kaine answered.

"Having just killed Lydia, they should already possess sufficient magic for whatever they intend to do. Why did they need more? And what's the point of holding onto Lydia's body? She's truly passed away, right?"

"That's enough about the sacrifices. I saw my daughter die. None of you saw it, but I did," Ether insisted. "This is pure evil—all of it. The Throatians' destination is Starlight Beach, no matter how they get there. We'll arrive before them and intercept them before they leave. Regardless of what else we might encounter on our journey, we must relentlessly push forward."

For the remainder of the day, they navigated the forest path, finding no signs of the Throatians. As night approached and fatigue set in, the Darians set up their camp. Overhead, a cloud haze blanketed the sky and obscured their view of the stars visible through the forest's canopy. Even though the soldiers had brought provisions, they hunted a deer and cooked it to conserve their resources—what they'd brought could never have fed over forty soldiers for a week. None had expected that it would take more than a day to catch up to the Throatians, especially since they were now without their horses.

The day's earlier rain made starting their several small campfires a challenge. After struggling to find dry tinder, they eventually gathered enough to keep warm through the night. Pausing there provided the first opportunity of the day to breathe and reflect on recent events. Shoulders still tense from waking on his bedchamber floor, Kaine rested on a large rock, gazing tiredly at the flames.

Beside him was Eisenbern, unfazed by sitting on the wet ground. His boots were off, and he was massaging his feet. "I wager you didn't foresee this chaos unfolding in your first days with the von Stonewall family."

Kaine turned away from the flames and stared sternly at him. "Is that supposed to be some kind of joke?"

"Not in the slightest," he clarified, "but I'm calling it what it is."

Kaine gave a quiet sigh. "Yeah. I guess that's what it is—crazy. The worst part of this is I'm not sure about what's going to happen next."

"It'll play out however Asura wills it," Eisenbern said solemnly. "But to state the obvious, eventually we're going to catch up to them, and there'll be a winner and a loser in the confrontation that follows. That's all there is to it. There's no point in worrying about anything else. Pressing onward is all we can do."

"How is it you appear unbothered by the risk?" Kaine asked. "Once we meet the Throatians, chances are we'll have to fight. After what they did to Lydia, there's no more room for fake pleasantries."

Eisenbern slid his feet back into his boots. "It's true that either of us could die—that's a fact we cannot deny. I signed up for this by joining the Purple Guard, and you're now in a similar role. The question I've since wondered is what happens once an ill fate catches up to me? My demise could happen any time. What matters most is how people will remember me—whether people will sing songs or if they'll only say some generic words that any other soldier might get when they pass away. I can't let myself die until I've done something worth remembering. Above all else, I don't want to be forgotten."

"You're being unduly critical of yourself," said Kaine. "If not for you, we wouldn't have the soldiers here. I'm no bard, but if you die before me, I'll write a song about how you rallied the troops that led to the defeat of the Throatians who betrayed us."

The nearby campfire crackled, and a small lone ember drifted up toward the sky against the continuous falling drizzles of rain. Moments later, its orange glow faded away and disappeared into the dark of night. "I just want to be remembered in a positive light, is all. Not forgotten or brushed aside as a faceless soldier."

Kaine smirked. "After how much we drank at the rehearsal dinner, I doubt anyone will forget us anytime soon."

Eisenbern chuckled. "As people get older, they think too much about life and death. It's better to keep it simple. Wish we had some beer to brood over it now, in fact."

Kaine held his tongue for a moment at the mention of alcohol and remembered the earlier times when he'd first stopped drinking it. "I've been down this trail of thought too many times already while I was at sea. The world back on land seems trivial the farther away you go. Remove society's illusions and you'll only have your soul left, pressed up against the void. I learned that the more complicated you make the idea of death, the harder it is to accept that it's coming to all of us someday."

Eisenbern held his invisible tankard up for a toast. "Do you know what you want people to say about you at your funeral yet, Boring Knight?"

"I haven't decided," Kaine said, pulling his legs closer to his chest and wrapping his arms around them. "But I plan on staying alive until I know for sure, no matter what happens next."

7
THE PRICE OF SORROW

Upon discovering the next morning that a Darian soldier had brought a homing pigeon, Ether von Stonewall asked Kaine to write a letter to the capital on his behalf. In his letter, Kaine updated the Darian council members on everything they'd encountered on the road so far. Kaine surmised that Ether lacked the emotional strength to write what had happened to Lydia. He also requested the council's aid in moving several ships from Wargonne to Starlight Beach. With favorable winds, the Darian Fleet could arrive days later and serve as a failsafe if anything went wrong with their plan to capture the Throatians.

The Darians continued their southeast trek for a handful of days. Aside from a nervous merchant who said she'd encountered no one else on the road, the rest of the ride was uneventful. On the seventh day since leaving Last Hope, the rain lifted, but smoke filled the horizon. Starlight Beach, typically a peaceful coastal town, was now in distress.

"It's under attack," Ether von Stonewall said. "Somehow, they beat us here—it must have been their magic. Prepare for battle!"

They entered through an archway of seashells and clay into the chaos of fearful civilians running through the streets. Embers and ash haunted the air like ghosts. Men ran by, carrying kitchen knives and shovels, searching down any alley or around any house that might be in trouble. It was all a horrific sight Kaine had never experienced before.

A sobbing woman ran up to them, eyeing the soldiers' armor. "My son! Did you see him? He's seventeen and dark-haired. They were chasing him. Did he escape town? Did you meet him on the roads?"

Eisenbern shook his head. "I'm sorry, we haven't seen him. No one has come from the direction opposite to the ocean for a few days now. But we'll keep our eyes open for him, I promise. Do you have shelter?"

"Th-thank you! Yes, I have a cellar. I'll lock it from inside."

He sent a guard to escort her home.

They scanned the streets, and though destruction

and mayhem had claimed the town, the perpetrators were nowhere to be seen. Whatever had happened there, they were too late to help. Finding another man hiding behind one of the market's stalls, Kaine pulled him out. "When did this all start?"

"I don't know. An hour and a half ago," the man cried. "They killed my family. Everyone's gone now."

"Did they have magic?" Eisenbern asked.

"What?"

"Magic," Kaine repeated. "Fire, lightning, ice—anything out of the ordinary."

"Just swords and sickles," the merchant said, "and they were foreigners, not Lucidians."

"We need to get to the docks," the king yelled.

His assumption was likely correct. If the massacre had started an hour and a half prior, it was probable that the Throatians had seen them coming and fled.

"Follow me," Kaine said. "I know these streets well!"

He maneuvered them through the chaotic streets, toward the ocean. By the time they reached the docks, three black Throatian ships were already about a quarter mile into the sea. He'd seen Throatian ships in his past jobs. Aside from having three red, fan-shaped sails instead of black ones, the royal ships were of the same build as Throatian merchant ships. Powerful winds surrounded the Throatians' island year-round, so their vessels didn't need oars or manual rowing capabilities. If the breezes at Starlight Beach remained calm, the Throatians would have a slow escape.

"We're late, but not by too much," the king said. "Since the Darian Fleet hasn't arrived from Wargonne, we need to commandeer some of the merchants' ships—they're our only hope for now."

The trader's vessels would lack the firepower needed to sink the Throatian ships. Aside from the basic defenses needed for warding off pirates, most captains invested little into ships' weapons. Both offensive and defensive upgrades were costly, and it was always better to flee a fight than to try winning one. In the Darians' case, they'd need to fight and likely board the enemy ships, too. Disabling their vessels or somehow cutting off their escape route was the most realistic option for avoiding direct combat.

After dismounting their horses, they continued down a wooden stairway into the docks. There, they quickly found two willing captains and divided themselves into two groups. Eisenbern would lead one vessel, Ether and Kaine the other.

"Take inventory of everything on board," the king directed a soldier. "We need to see what we've got at our disposal."

"I say this with respect, King von Stonewall," the

ship's captain said, "but what do you mean by disposal? My cargo isn't cheap. Can't we just chase them without attacking until your military arrives? Throwing barrels at them won't do much damage."

"Whatever happens, we'll compensate you well for it," Ether said. "My friend Kaine here used to be a trader on a ship like this one. He'll ensure you get your fair share once this is all done. Just let us borrow your ships."

"All right then." The captain patted his pocket while failing to hold back a grin.

The guard the king had sent below deck returned a moment later. "They have several crates of peppers, salts, perfumes, toy dolls, and textiles."

"Excellent," Ether said. "The perfumes are flammable. We can throw their bottles at the sides of their ships as we approach, aiming for places their crew can't easily reach. A few fire arrows from our archers will light them, and then they'll burn from the bottom up. The problem is that they still have Lydia's body. We have to retrieve her first."

"Boarding their ships is the only way to accomplish that," Kaine pointed out. "It's not a smart move —we're too outnumbered."

"We're wasting time," Ether said. "Let's get going now and we'll keep planning during our chase."

Launching from the docks, they began their pursuit. As the two ships followed the Throatian vessels, still painfully far from attack range, Eisenbern remained aboard Kaine and Ether's for the time being to continue their discussion.

"As we approach the Throatians, we'll need to break formation and split up," the captain said to Kaine and Ether. "The enemy will surround us otherwise."

"Since your ship lacks proper weaponry, you're limited to using any flammable substance you can throw," Eisenbern said. His own vessel had a ramming bow. "Let me lead the attack, since I can poke them. I'll try stabbing their ships' waterline first and you can follow up if that doesn't work. There's no point in risking running out of perfume when I can ram."

The king chewed his lip, lost in thought for a moment.

"My apologies, but I must also agree with Kaine," Eisenbern added. "Boarding is far too risky. We lack the numbers for direct combat with the Throatians. They have three ships and we have two. We should board only if we can reduce their numbers or if our reinforcements from Wargonne arrive."

The king banged his fist on the ship's railing. "I hate it, but you're correct," he growled. "I can't let my anguish affect my judgment. Better the odds first, and then we'll try to save Lydia once we've gained the upper hand."

Eisenbern nodded curtly. "We'll do it with honor," he declared, as the other ship moved in closer, and he laid a plank between the vessels to let a portion of the troops join Kaine and Ether. Satisfied that everyone had optimally divided themselves amongst the two vessels, Eisenbern gave Kaine a nod as he boarded the one he'd be leading. "That leaves thirty-two of us here, including the merchant's crew at the oars. Should anything go wrong, we'll jump off and try making our way back to you," he promised as he kicked the plank back over to Kaine's ship.

"Good luck and may Asura's grace protect you!" the king said. He waved farewell to Eisenbern, then turned to the soldiers. "We've traveled for a week, hunting down those who promised to become our allies. They've murdered my daughter, butchered our horses, and pillaged Starlight Beach. It's unforgivable! Do not let them escape!" He drew his sword and pointed it toward the Throatian ships ahead.

With oars flailing at full speed, Eisenbern's ship began closing the gap to the Throatians, slowly yet determinedly. Whispers of sea breeze swept against Kaine's cheeks as he watched the gales pushing the vessels farther away from Starlight Beach. Eisenbern's ship then raised its oars, conserving energy.

"How long do you think it will take us to catch them?" Ether asked.

"We're at the mercy of the wind," Kaine said. "Among all the ships, only Eisenbern's vessel has oars. Once he rams them or forces them to change course, the Throatians will have to slow down, and that will be our opportunity to take them. Our ability to maneuver will make all the difference."

The king squinted at the horizon. "So, if the wind changes direction or calms, then only Eisenbern's ship will have full control. Perfect."

"Not exactly," Kaine said. "It will still be three ships against one, and we don't know what weapons the Throatians have. Or magic."

"Ah, magic. Of course."

"You don't think they have it?"

"I'm assuming they would have used it by now if they did."

"If you're correct, then defeating them will be easier," Kaine said. "The alternative is that they are waiting for the most strategic time to use it. Still, it will take some time before we catch up to them and know for sure."

"I suspect we'll settle everything within a day.

You should rest for now," the king said. "I'll need you at full strength."

"Yes, sir," Kaine said. "You should rest too."

"If only I could," Ether said. "I haven't rested right since the day before the wedding. I can't… not until we bring the Throatians to justice. Pain doesn't sleep."

Kaine nodded, keeping himself from saying anything else. There was no way he could comprehend losing a daughter. Kaine bid the king goodnight, went below deck, and found himself a bed. Like all the previous ships he'd served on, the bunk beds were for quick shifts. He planned on resting for a few hours, then would go above deck to check whether they were closer to the Throatians.

Lying in his bunk, he couldn't help letting his mind revisit the night before the wedding. When he had last seen Lydia, she'd met him in the cemetery and given him the letter and wine. Though it had only been days, it felt like months ago. Lydia had seemed content with how her future would play out and all her efforts seemed focused on preventing conflict with the Throatians. She'd clearly feared their magic, so there must have been more details within the memories she'd absorbed from the Asche royal family than what she'd told him. Still, were the powers of the God Stones stronger than what the Throatians had at their disposal?

Ether von Stonewall seemed familiar with the God Stones' abilities; perhaps he could have guided her to use them if he had known the situation she was in. Regardless, it was possible she, like her father, believed that such power should remain a secret. Mind reading was a powerful ability on its own, but if the von Stonewall family had four stones with similar capabilities, they could defeat anyone who opposed them. Perhaps there wasn't enough time. Then again, it sounded like there were more stones out there that could pose just as big a threat. How many more stones existed in total? And why weren't the Throatians using their supposed magic?

Engulfed in his thoughts, Kaine succumbed to sleep. He rested, comforted by the ship's familiar rocking for almost an hour, before someone patted him awake.

"You're Kaine Khalia, right?" a Darian guard asked.

"Yes," he said, blinking his eyes and reaching for his sword. "What's happening?"

"We haven't caught up to them yet, but there's something you should see. The king sent for you. It's bad."

Kaine sat up, fastening his sword and sheath to his belt.

"Lead the way."

Both of them ascended to the main deck. As the sun set on the horizon, the wind and rain held steady. Eisenbern's ship was now positioned halfway between their vessel and those of the Throatians. Everything seemed normal until Kaine spotted three faint orange glows in the distance.

"Why are the Throatian ships already aflame?" Kaine demanded. "Did Eisenbern ignite them and retreat?"

"No," said the guard, handing him a telescope. "Look more closely."

Kaine pointed the telescope toward one of the Throatian vessels. Each ship hoisted a burning body from a long metal pole jutting out from their sterns. Chained by their feet and swinging upside down, each individual was aflame from head to toe. Sacrifices—one per vessel.

Lowering the telescope, Kaine frowned. "But who are they? Are Throatians killing each other for good luck?"

"They're hostages," bellowed the king's voice from behind. He strode across the ship's deck, his eyes locked on Kaine. "Now we know why the Throatians didn't sneak aboard their ships quietly;

they brewed up chaos before they left so they could abduct victims. Those are residents of Starlight Beach."

"I'm amazed they had the time to do all that," Kaine replied. "I can't believe it. The man at Starlight Beach said the attack lasted about an hour. Was that enough time to pillage the entire town and collect hostages too?"

"It doesn't matter," said Ether. "They've done it."

Kaine grimaced. "Then we'll send them to the black sands of Tornaa or die trying."

They could do little to make good on their promise that night. With the winds remaining unchanged, they made little progress toward closing the distance with the enemy ships. Meanwhile, each of the Throatian ships, once every hour, cut their victims loose and replaced them with more sacrifices. Screams competed with the roar of the ocean waves, fading into silence each time.

"One's a child!" the captain exclaimed as Kaine's stomach lurched. "They're burning someone's baby girl!"

Eight more hours of night remained before sunrise, and there was nothing they could do.

Once daylight arrived, the burning of hostages stopped, although only temporarily. Over the next several days, the wind persisted the same as the kingdoms continued their journeys in stalemate.

Each night, additional hostages were hanged, burned, and left to die upside down, suspended from the ships. Kaine wondered if the Throatians truly believed in their sacrifices or if their intention was only to agitate the Darians.

"How many more people do you think they have?" the captain of the ship asked Kaine on the sixth night.

"As many people as they believed necessary to return home." Kaine looked toward the horizon. "You're familiar with these waters, right, Captain?"

"Aye."

"Would you agree that we're about a day from the Throatian island? I've gone back and forth on this route before, though not under these circumstances. I've lost track of where we are."

"You're not far off," the captain said. "I'd wager we're about a day or two from getting there."

"Either way, we are running out of time. There's no way we can challenge them if they get close enough to their island. If they sent a bird home and requested other ships to come, we may end up facing more than just these three."

"Eisenbern should row ahead and ram them now then," the captain remarked. "It's our best bet for sinking one of their ships. The other bastards might not turn around in time to do anything. The wind is against them."

"Let's ask the king."

They presented the idea to Ether and warned him that time was running short.

"Then we should do this soon," he said. "Blow the horn at sunrise so Eisenbern will know to start. We shouldn't do this blinded by the night."

At dawn the following day, their ship sounded its signal horn and Eisenbern's ship began rowing full speed again. Preparing to intercept the Throatian ships, it maneuvered to the left and arced into a collision course.

"Have you ever seen a ship ram another?" Ether asked Kaine.

"Never on purpose, sir. I've only witnessed it during storms when ships were traveling too close together and lost control."

"So, is there a good chance the Throatian ship will sink?"

"Yes, the ramming structure is a heavy and durable metal," Kaine explained. "As long as Eisenbern stabs at a good speed and angle, he shouldn't damage his own ship."

The Throatian ships quickly recognized Eisenbern's intentions and adjusted their courses to flee from him, which put them solidly against the wind; an advantage for the Purple Guard leader, already close as he was to them. His beak edged closer to the nearest Throatian ship, pointed toward its stern. In a last-ditch effort to slip away, the Throatian ship changed direction again, but it was too late; Eisenbern pierced the waterline at its rear. Wood boards creaked and snapped as the metal ram pushed its way through the enemy ship. The wounded boat tilted downwards, dipping slightly below the water's surface without rising again.

"It's bound for the ocean's bottom, that one," the captain said. "She's nailed in a pretty critical spot. I wager she'll be under within five minutes."

"Excellent," declared the king. "Let's regroup with Eisenbern. The remaining two Throatian ships are rerouting to rescue their survivors. We'll intercept them."

Eisenbern's ship attempted to reverse direction and paddle away, but the sinking ship rotated with it.

"He's stuck," Kaine shouted. "If he can't reverse in time, the other ship will pull him under!"

"Black sand," the captain said. "What's more important to you, my king? Saving the other ship or attacking the enemy? We might only have the opportunity to do one."

"Our priority is to save our people," stated Ether von Stonewall. "We'll not let the ocean bury them with the Throatians. I won't mix the graves of my people with cold-blooded murderers."

They pressed forward toward Eisenbern's

ensnared vessel. To break the two vessels free of each other, they would need to crash their ship into the connection point. If the king's ship became damaged, boarding Eisenbern's vessel was the last option. The oars of his ship were crucial; without them, their group could become trapped at sea for weeks and there were not nearly enough provisions to keep everyone alive for that long.

Before they could reach the entangled vessels, Throatians leapt from the deck, using Eisenbern's ram as a makeshift bridge to infiltrate his ship. Using hooks and ropes, they ascended the bow and reached the other deck in seconds.

"He's in trouble," Kaine yelled to the crew. "We must board Eisenbern's ship and help him!"

"But it's going to sink!" the captain said. "They're better off grabbing some planks and jumping. Both ships are going under if we don't break their grasp of each other."

"Maintain course for ramming with our ship," the king ordered. "We'll escape to Eisenbern's vessel once we've saved it from sinking."

By the time they approached, Eisenbern and Harkbin were already clashing blades. Although Harkbin towered over Eisenbern, the leader of the Purple Guard had the greater agility. With various jumps and rolls, he easily avoided the slashes of Harkbin's claymore. Eisenbern's skills had improved since the last time Kaine had witnessed him fight, several years prior.

Their ship collided with the two intertwined vessels and successfully severed the connection. Eisenbern's ship pulled away unharmed, but the hull of the king's ship suffered damage; its boards caved inwards, and the entire deck shuddered with the impact and sudden onboarding of water. The impact had caused a rupture beneath the ocean's surface. The hole might have been small, but the resulting damage was catastrophic; it would only be a matter of time before Kaine and Ether's ship would descend with the Throatians'.

They steered their slowly submerging vessel alongside Eisenbern's, laid down planks as makeshift bridges, then plunged into the fray. As the enemy ship submerged next to them, Kaine deflected an enemy's blade and retaliated with a swing of his own weapon, dismembering the Throatian's arm. Luckily, most of the Throatians' armor left the areas near their shoulders exposed.

As the soldier crumpled to the ground, Kaine pivoted and crouched behind another Throatian already locked in combat with a Darian guard. Taking advantage of his enemy's lack of awareness, he stabbed him in the calf, breaking the Throatian's concentration and giving the other Darian soldier an easy finish. The soldier thanked him as Kaine moved on to fight his next foe.

A sudden force jolted Kaine from behind, denting his armor and catapulting him over the railing to the deck below. With his lungs emptied, he flung his hands out desperately in front of him as he tumbled down the stairs into the storage room below. His head thudded against the wooden floor at the base of the steps. He recovered his breath as a woman yelled something in a language he did not understand. Urith, the Throatian Queen, stood at the top entrance, wielding a bloody war hammer. She wore scaly textured clothing, most likely skinned from a large reptile and dyed black, but it didn't seem to be armor. Kaine scrambled to his feet and grabbed his sword from the ground.

Drawing a painful breath, he found himself barely able to speak, the wind knocked out of him. "You killed Princess Lydia!"

"Yes."

She raised the hammer above her shoulders, bent her knees, then threw herself down toward him. Kaine pivoted to the left, avoiding her blow, then swung his blade horizontally and sliced through her ineffective leather clothing—right between her ribs. The cut was shallow, but enough to make her yelp in pain. Using one hand, she lashed her hammer at him and knocked the sword from his grasp. His blade fell to the ground between them, out of reach as long as she had her hammer.

Urith cursed in her native tongue, holding her wound with one hand and her hammer in the other. Kaine cautiously retreated up the stairs; gaining higher ground would provide temporary safety. Unfortunately, she wouldn't let him take the opportunity. With her hammer pointed at him, she shouted and charged. Kaine tucked his chin into his chest and threw his entire body weight down at her, using gravity to his advantage. He blocked as a loud clack, dry and hollow—as if two rocks were being smashed together—echoed from his left arm. As the hammer drove forward, the bones within his bracer shattered into a thousand pieces, but the block saved his life. The collision knocked them both to the ground, causing Urith to drop her weapon as well.

Kaine's left arm hung limp and throbbing. He wanted to scream until his throat curled raw, but for now his right hand, still free, instinctively grabbed his sword. Armed once again, he quickly pierced the Throatian Queen's chest as hard as he could. She screamed and tried to grab Kaine's blade, but he leaned into his sword to keep her from pulling it out. The image of the monster he'd slain in the forest flashed in his mind as he dizzily held his ground. As time seemed to hold still, he continued pushing forward until Urith's head and massive upper body finally thudded to the floor.

Drawing a deep breath, he used his entire weight to tug his sword free from her chest. With his arm still throbbing, he removed his bracer to reveal the purple, swollen limb. Urith's weapon had rendered his arm useless, the shock from the fight temporarily dulling the full extent of his pain. Still somewhat disoriented, he cast a last glance at her, then went back upstairs. The battle on the deck had concluded and Harkbin Asche was on his knees, facing Eisenbern. Ether von Stonewall stood behind Eisenbern, pointing his blade at the other Throatian soldiers, whose hands were bound in surrender. Dead warriors from both sides of the battle littered the deck.

Having captured the Throatian king, the Darian Kingdom now possessed leverage, but the wind unexpectedly changed direction. Kaine gazed into the distance, spotting the remaining two Throatian ships closing in on them.

"YOU'RE GOING TO HAVE THEM BRING ME LYDIA'S body," Ether von Stonewall commanded the Throatian King, unconcerned about the reinforcements. "Then I'll see you and your men safely back to your ship. After that, you're never to return to the Darian Kingdom again. Do you understand?"

Harkbin nodded in silent agreement.

"Good," the Darian King replied. "Eisenbern, take Harkbin over to where the other ships can see him and have him hold up the white flag."

"Yes, sir," Eisenbern said, wiping blood off his temple. He signaled with his blade for Harkbin to stand.

"Has anyone seen Kaine?" Ether asked.

"I'm here," Kaine called out, stepping over bodies and blood to approach.

"Are you all right?" He pointed to Kaine's loosely hanging arm.

"I've seen better days," Kaine replied, then leaned in so he could whisper. "I defeated Urith. She's below deck. I had no choice but to kill her."

The king nodded. "Keep that knowledge to yourself for now and stand by for your next orders."

Prince Thane, who'd apparently abstained from the battle, peered at them from the deck of the closest intact vessel.

"You've bested us for today," Thane said. "We'll pay you an appropriate amount of gold for my father and mother."

Ether von Stonewall stepped forward. "We don't

want money. Give me my daughter's body along with all your food and supplies."

"Done," Prince Thane replied. "But where is my mother?"

"We don't know," Ether said. "I haven't seen her since you threw me out of your carriage."

The Throatian prince studied him for a moment. "She boarded your ship. I'm sure of it."

"If neither of us sees her, then she's not here," Ether said. "Even if we bested her, we would have kept her alive as leverage."

Clutching his broken arm, Kaine held his silence. His effectiveness in battle would be null if the Throatians discovered Urith's death and resumed the fight because of it. Only his adrenaline prevented him from screaming out from the pain radiating throughout his shattered, dominant limb.

"Fine," Thane said. "My wife for my father and my men's lives for our supplies."

Ether scowled at the prince's words. Without a doubt, he would annul his daughter's marriage once they returned home.

"First, I want Lydia and the supplies," Ether demanded. "I'm sure you'll understand that I don't find your people trustworthy."

"Okay," Thane said. His ship came closer to theirs and tossed some ropes with which to bind the vessels. A moment later, Throatian soldiers carried the first load of supplies over to the Darians. As the Throatians returned to their ship to collect the second load, Ether von Stonewall approached Harkbin and made him kneel in front of him. Behind Harkbin, Eisenbern stood guard.

"So, your magic was merely an illusion after all," the king said.

Harkbin coughed several times. "Not all magic is seen, you fool."

"But apparently, all of your magic is useless," Ether countered. "It couldn't save you from getting captured, nor could it save your ships from being at our mercy. Either your god doesn't exist, or he believes in the justice of the Darian Kingdom!"

Harkbin snorted. "If your only intention is to taunt me, stop now. Your inflated ego will wither once you lose everything."

Eisenbern stepped closer to the prisoner. "I want to know who else wanted Princess Lydia sacrificed. Was it just your family, or were there others back in your homeland involved in this monstrosity?"

He presented a fair point. Should only the Asche family and their immediate followers had been involved in human sacrifices, there might not be a need to go to war with their country later. His question was simple, yet enough to hint at whether there would be a war with the entire Throatian Kingdom later.

"Our god tells us what to do, and we do it in his name," Harkbin said. "We do not know why he gave us this mission or what should happen afterward, but all that happened was part of his plan for us. Our country stands united regardless of what happens to me. Every sacrifice is for the greater good, no matter the cost to us mere mortals."

"You should have thought more carefully," Kaine said, stepping forward. "Your choice in performing sacrifices will bring about grave consequences for you and your people. Not only did you incite the wrath of an entire kingdom, but you murdered someone who you invited into your family. Lydia didn't deserve to die and everyone knows it."

Harkbin scoffed. "As though you are qualified to preach on the absolutes of good and evil in our universe. Only our god knows what is real. Only our god has a grand plan to free us into a world of riches and prosperity."

Kaine locked eyes with Harkbin, observing the volatile mix of fervor and fear in his stare. There was no magical reward from his god, yet the Throatian king only had his religion to lean on.

"Burn in the black sands of Tornaa," Kaine said. "Lydia was worth more than your entire family combined."

"Enough," Eisenbern barked. "Shut up, both of you."

They watched in tense silence as the Throatians offloaded the last of the supplies. Having set down the last box of food and water, the Throatians then carried Lydia over to the ship. Enshrouded in cloth, her body was unrecognizable, making it hard to confirm if it was truly Lydia.

"Kaine," uttered Ether. "Check if it's her."

Kaine suspected he couldn't bear to see Lydia's body, but he approached the Throatians waiting at the other ship and knelt next to the bundled corpse. Using his uninjured hand, he peeled back the cotton flap, revealing Lydia's pale face. He replaced the cloth quickly and averted his eyes.

"It's her," Kaine said.

Ether choked on his words. "Guards, bring me my daughter."

Four guards proceeded to where Kaine was hunched over and delicately hoisted Lydia's body. With somber expressions, they transported her to their king, following his order.

"I'm so sorry, my daughter," Ether whispered to the wrapped bundle in front of him. He then looked toward the Darian guards. "Kill the prisoners."

"Are you certain, my king?" one soldier asked.

"Do it."

A moment later, all the Throatian soldiers were face down on the deck and lifeless. The Darians stood over their fallen foes, their swords stained with crimson, exchanging anxious glances amongst themselves.

"Move, Eisenbern," Ether von Stonewall said, motioning his sword away from Harkbin.

Kaine's mouth fell open as he approached. No good would come by killing the Throatian king. Surely Ether knew this too and was just using the situation as some kind of strategic leverage against Prince Thane. Chances were that Ether would return Harkbin as a last chance of good faith toward preventing a war. It wasn't tasteful, but it would show the Throatians to think twice before sacrificing anyone in the future.

"Stop it," Eisenbern commanded. "You're breaking your deal. Killing their crew was enough. Have you lost all your honor?"

"I lost everything when they took my daughter from me," Ether said, tears creeping down his face. "These Throatians are the lowest kinds of filth. It doesn't matter if it's their religion or how they get magic. Their sins are too many."

Eisenbern's shoulders slumped, resigned. "If this is what you wish, my king, then so be it." He moved out from behind Harkbin and swapped places with the king.

Ether took a knee behind Harkbin, pulling a knife that was strapped to his ankle and pressing it against the Throatian king's neck. Across the deck stood Prince Thane, not moving or reacting. Kaine couldn't help but wonder why Thane wasn't trying to stop the situation from unfolding. Perhaps the prince saw through Ether's threats as well?

"You needlessly took my people captive and burned them aboard your ships," Ether said. "Your crew paid their price. Now, since you killed Lydia, it's only fair I take someone important from you too."

Kaine hastened over to the heated exchange between Ether and Eisenbern. The king wasn't trying to trick Thane or gain leverage at all—it was clear now he really did want to kill Harkbin.

"Don't do this, sir," Kaine interrupted. "We all agree the Throatians are wrong, but if you kill Harkbin, you're going to start a war. Lydia wouldn't want this. Xander and Kira wouldn't want it either."

The dagger trembling at Harkbin's neck betrayed Ether's struggle to decide. Surely Ether would see reason once he calmed down. Kaine looked over to Prince Thane, standing nonchalantly on his ship. He either hid his emotions well or didn't care his father was in danger.

"I need to protect my children," Ether said. "Can't you see it? The war started when they murdered Lydia." His knife lowered ever so slightly.

"Put down your weapon, my king," Eisenbern pleaded. "If you don't want to let him go, we can bring him back with us as a prisoner for now. We can put him on trial and handle this the proper way."

Tears carved their way down Ether's wrinkled face as his gaze wavered between Eisenbern and Kaine.

"They didn't allow Lydia to change her fate," he said, then jammed the knife into Harkbin's throat. Blood spattered across the wood as the Throatian king's body thudded to the deck.

"What have you done?" Kaine wheezed as the king's blade clattered to the ground. He wanted to punch the king, but his arm throbbed with such intensity that no alternative action remained viable. The searing sensation enveloping his entire limb resembled the torment of submerging it in boiling water.

Ether remained on his knees, quickly sweeping his gaze over his Darian guards and the Throatians on the other ship. He stared down at his hands, transfixed by the blood staining his palms.

"I apologize. I-I shouldn't have—" his voice died in his throat. Silently, he rose to his feet and moved towards the stairs leading below deck. As he descended into the storage room, a faint moan echoed. Thane, however, merely observed, his expression unreadable. It was impossible to determine whether he was in shock or oddly indifferent about his father's demise.

"Guards, return the Throatian king to his ship," Eisenbern ordered. "It's the least we can do."

Kaine slid his blade back into its sheath. "Do the same for the Throatian Queen. She's by the stairs below deck. Bring her carefully and respectfully."

"What?" Eisenbern murmured in disbelief. "Urith Asche is dead too? But Ether said he didn't—"

"I killed her in self-defense. She almost got me. Her war hammer broke my arm. If we'd fought for another minute, I would be dead."

Unexpectedly, the skies turned from gray to black, and a downpour heavier than Kaine had ever witnessed started. He instinctively raised his unharmed arm to shield his face. Each raindrop stung like a sharp needle piercing his skin. Thunder roared in the proximity, causing the entire ship to quiver. As sudden as it was intense, the storm posed a threat to everyone on the ships.

Abandoning their king and queen's bodies, the Throatian soldiers quickly removed the ropes connecting the two kingdom's ships and fled below their deck. Seconds after the Throatian people disappeared, a heavy wind pushed directly from the sky, generating a small tidal wave where it hit the sea. The waters forced the two Throatian ships away from the Darians', while fresh waves emerged, churning and swiveling the vessels. The Throatian ships turned and faced their homeland, and a final gust descended from the sky, separating the two kingdoms even further. Once the Darians and Throatians were nearly out of sight from each other, the storm died as instantaneously as it appeared. The sky was gray and calm again.

"What in the black sands of Tornaa?" Eisenbern wondered aloud. "Was that Throatian magic?"

"It was only a flash storm," Kaine said. "And it couldn't have been Throatian magic. We'd be dead otherwise. Besides, Thane didn't wait to collect his parents' bodies. He fled from the raging weather too."

Ether von Stonewall returned to the ship's deck, commanding everyone to congregate around him. He stared at his feet as everyone approached. Kaine briefly counted the number of people still alive. The count fell short of twenty.

"Everyone, I'm sorry I've failed you," the king said. "Today, I paid the price of my sorrow with my honor, and I regret what I did. Please work with me to put this all behind us. Scour our wrecked ship for any remaining supplies or resources. Once Eisenbern deems it clear, move the dead, both the Darians and Throatians alike, and pour the perfume over their bodies. We'll burn that ship and let them rest at sea. Today, only Lydia will return home with us."

8

THE ROSE OF THE DARIAN KINGDOM

The Darian survivors sailed back toward Starlight Beach for three days before the main fleet from Wargonne came to their rescue. Ether von Stonewall ordered them to sail together to Starlight Beach, planning to return everyone to Last Hope from there. Throughout their journey at sea, King Ether largely kept to himself, only conversing with the crew when necessary. He stayed below deck in his cabin and, once back on land, switched to secluding himself within his carriage. Three weeks after the battle, they reached Last Hope and held Lydia's long overdue funeral the following day. Ether buried his firstborn daughter within the cemetery near the castle, close to where Kaine had secretly received the letter and the wine from her.

At Lydia's wake, Councilman Merdel introduced Kaine to Xander and Kira. The young Prince Xander kept his chin up, uttering a brief hello and avoiding eye contact. Kira couldn't say a word as tears streamed down her sniffling face.

"Could you watch over them for a bit, Kaine?" Merdel asked. "I have to go attend to something back at the castle. I wish you all were meeting under different circumstances, but it is what it is."

"Of course, Councilman. I won't let them out of my sight," Kaine replied. Taking care of the von Stonewall children was his job. He squatted down to level himself with the young prince and princess. "I'm so sorry about what happened to Lydia. I know you don't know who I am, but I was her friend. She cared very much about both of you. Please be strong for her."

Xander looked away as Kira continued to cry uncontrollably. There was no shortcut for processing what had taken place within their family. Kaine recalled Lydia's plea for him to fill the void she would leave behind. "Kira, would you like a hug?" he asked.

She instinctively moved toward him, and he embraced her with his good arm. The one that Urith shattered remained wrapped in a sling and would likely stay that way for months. "Everything will be okay," he said as she clung to him.

He saw Xander staring over at them. "Do you want to join us, Xander?"

The prince scuffed the ground with the sole of his shoe, shifting it against the dirt.

"No."

"That's fine. You don't have to. I understand that I'm a stranger." Kaine let go of Kira as she momentarily stopped crying and moved her bushy brown hair out of her eyes. Her skin was pale white and held the faintest hint of pink on her cheeks—exactly like Lydia's.

Observing their surroundings, Kaine noticed that none of the attendees seemed to pay attention or acknowledge the three of them. Everyone else was engulfed in their own conversations, unaware or purposefully avoiding contact with the prince and princess who'd just lost their older sister.

Xander's face filled with curiosity and wonder. "You're the one they call the Boring Knight, aren't you?"

"Yes, but I'm not fond of that name."

Xander chuckled. "Yeah, it's stupid. You killed a monster; you should get a better one than that."

Kaine nodded. "I would if I could. The title wasn't my choice."

"Queen Killer has a better ring to it," Xander proposed. "After all, you defeated the Throatian queen during the battle."

Kaine shook his head. "I'm not sure I like that name either. Maybe we can think of something else later."

For the first time, Xander met Kaine's eyes. The young prince's hazel brown eyes sparkled with admiration. "Thank you for getting rid of her. She deserved it."

"Fate determined it should be that way, I suppose. I didn't intend to kill Urith; I had no choice. She attacked me; I was simply defending myself. When you grow up, you might find yourself in a similar situation. Always try to negotiate with your enemies first, if possible. Killing people only leads to more bloodshed."

Xander nodded. "As long as the bad people are the ones dying, then it's okay."

"Maybe," Kaine replied. "Sometimes it's hard to tell who is good and who is bad. Be careful when you decide."

Finally, Kira spoke. "Are all the Throatians bad people, Kaine?"

Before he could answer, Councilman Merdel returned to them.

"Greetings again, everyone," Merdel said. "False alarm at the castle, so I ended up not having to walk all the way back there. Xander and Kira, are you both doing okay? Do you like Kaine Khalia so far?"

"Yes, he is a powerful knight," Xander said. His sister simply nodded.

"I'm glad that's the case," Merdel replied. "The three of you are going to be spending a lot of time together. But for now, I'm supposed to return you to your father. Come with me, children."

The prince and princess approached him, each taking hold of one of his hands. They departed from Kaine's side, leaving him in solitude for the rest of Lydia's wake. Despite having known Lydia for only a few days, the circumstances of her death cut him deeply. The worst of the events had passed, and with Lydia put to rest, the Darian kingdom could begin moving forward from the aftermath of what people were calling "The Wedding of the Torn Rose".

After the wake, Eisenbern needed to return to the Leila Kingdom, and Kaine went to send him off.

"I knew the Throatians wanted to murder Lydia before her wedding," Kaine confessed as he and his friend walked toward the stables. "I lacked the evidence, but I feel like I didn't do enough to stop everything from happening."

"There wasn't anything you really could have

done without jeopardizing yourself or Lydia," Eisenbern said. "In the absence of solid proof, most would assume you had ulterior motives or were crazy. What you did after the wedding brought some level of justice for Lydia, though."

"Yes, I suppose," Kaine said, still wavering. "But do you believe the Leila Kingdom will join with the Darian Kingdom if war breaks out?"

"I expect so—after all, our kingdoms are sisters," Eisenbern reminded him. "My letter to Queen Blanche explains everything we saw after the wedding and at sea. I'm sure she'll have an opinion on all of this, too, once we get the chance to discuss in person. Regardless of whether war is starting, preparation is essential."

"The king is wasting no time in planning for it," Kaine said. "He summoned me to meet with him this afternoon."

"By the way," Eisenbern said. "I trust you'll make frequent visits to the Leila Kingdom, given your new position here. It'd been too long since we last saw each other. In case you were wondering, I'm frankly insulted that it took a chance encounter in the woods with another kingdom's princess for us to finally catch up."

"Sorry it took so long," Kaine said. Eisenbern was right, and Lydia had been too. Kaine also owed it to his parents to visit their graves. "Returning home will be a priority. I assure you."

"You'd better," Eisenbern laughed. "It will please Queen Blanche once she learns I encountered you on my trip. You were the last person I expected to see here. Anyway, I hope your new job with Prince Xander and Princess Kira goes well."

"Thank you, Eisenbern. It's been an interesting start since I arrived here, but I'm hopeful for the future."

Eisenbern offered his hand. "So, this is goodbye for now, then. Seriously though, don't question yourself about what happened with Princess Lydia. You made the right decisions."

"Thank you again. I'll try not to let it weigh on me too much."

"Great," Eisenbern said. "Hang in there and remember what you're staying alive for!" With that, he rode out through the main gate.

Now alone, Kaine roamed through the capital back to the royal castle and returned to his bedchamber. Lydia's funeral had mentally exhausted him; taking a brief nap would help revitalize his mind before his meeting with the king. He drew back his sheets and listened to the crackling of the firewood. Once he'd almost fallen asleep, someone knocked at his door.

"Just a moment," Kaine said as he got out of his

bed and straightened the blankets and duvet again. He pulled a shirt over his head and opened the door.

A woman of dark complexion, with long, graying hair, extended a warm greeting. In her hands, she carried a small journal and quill. She wore a formal blue robe, and a leather satchel hung from one shoulder, dangling at her waist. She pursed her lips as she studied him.

"You are Kaine Khalia, the newly appointed retainer of the prince and princess, correct?"

"Yes," Kaine replied. "And you are?"

"My apologies," she said. "We haven't properly met yet. I am Iris Thorne, the Darian Councilwoman of Internal Affairs. There are a few questions I'd like you to answer about the night before the wedding if you have time now."

"Sure."

"My records indicate you were absent from the ceremony," Iris stated. "May I ask why?"

Kaine's gaze froze as he could only feel his heart beating.

"I overslept," he said. "It pains me terribly that I missed the wedding. I swear it."

Iris nodded and scribbled in her notebook. "Hm, I see. And why did you oversleep?"

"I have a problem sometimes," Kaine said. "When I'm anxious, I sometimes overindulge in alcohol. The night before the wedding, I drank some wine. I didn't realize how strong the alcohol was, so I passed out on my floor. This won't happen again or affect my future duties, I promise."

She continued jotting down notes. "And roughly how much wine do you estimate you consumed that night?"

Kaine knew he'd had a drinking problem in the past, and this wasn't the first time he'd gone overboard from having too much alcohol. In those past instances, he'd barely felt drunk at all until he reached his limit—then came the vomiting and passing out. That night, Lydia's gift was the last piece of cargo needed to sink his boat. Still, how could he explain it without sounding like he was an irresponsible drunkard?

"I drank one bottle of wine, but it was about half the size of a typical bottle," Kaine said. "It was about the size of a tankard or so. It wasn't a lot."

Iris nodded at him. "I believe you. In fact, could you confirm whether this bottle contains the wine you consumed that night?" She reached into her leather satchel and pulled out the bottle Lydia had gifted him in the graveyard.

"Yes, that's it," Kaine said. "I'm sorry if missing the wedding caused trouble. I promise I won't drink too much like this ever again."

She gave him a slight smile—as if she wanted to laugh, but her position required her to remain neutral. "Oh, I'm not here to punish you. I'm only collecting facts. It puzzled me you'd missed the wedding but were the first to announce the Throatians' intentions of murdering Princess Lydia, so I ordered a search of your chambers. The wine bottle and vomit on the floor prompted me to investigate what you'd been drinking. Someone wanted you to miss the wedding and spiked your wine with a small amount of Death's Whisper."

"What?" Kaine exclaimed. "Someone wanted me to die?"

"Death's Whisper is a long-term sleeping agent," Iris explained. "A normal dose will put you to sleep for several days and promote your body's self-healing. There was only enough of it in your wine for a long night's sleep."

Thus, Lydia's "gift" had been intended to prevent him from interfering with her the next morning.

"Black sand," Kaine muttered. He'd been blaming himself for drinking too much and oversleeping, but it was truly Lydia's fault all along.

"Hm?" Iris inquired, her eyes meeting his. "I can sense you've recalled something. Where did you get this wine?"

Kaine quickly invented a lie, unsure if he fully trusted Iris yet. "Urith Asche, the Throatian Queen, gave me the wine as thanks for saving Lydia from the monster in the forest."

"I see." Iris nodded. "That makes sense. If Urith had suspicions about your knowledge of the Throatian's plans, poisoning you would be a logical course of action. However, her choice of weapon is indeed surprising. In the future, Kaine Khalia, be cautious of those from whom you accept drinks."

"Oh, I will," Kaine replied. "I definitely will."

LATER THAT DAY, KAINE HEADED TO THE THRONE room for his meeting with the king. The guard guided him to the entryway, informing him that no formal announcement was necessary; Kaine could enter whenever he felt ready. Kaine was unaccustomed to entering the throne room without announcement. Perhaps the usual formalities had been suspended in light of recent events. Sheepishly, he used his entire body to push open the massive doors. Taken aback by the creaks of the ancient wood, Kaine noted the absence of any staff, servants, or guards awaiting his arrival. Ether von Stonewall sat alone on the crystal throne, scribbling in a notebook, and looked up to watch Kaine enter. It was the first time they'd talked alone since defeating the Throatians weeks ago.

"Thank you for coming here on such brief notice," Ether said. "I apologize for not having any food or wine to offer you."

Kaine approached him and knelt. "It's my pleasure, sir. My king summoned me, and so I came. But if I may ask, where is everybody?"

The king's face appeared thinner and paler than Kaine remembered. It was likely the king had lost his appetite to mourning. The stress of losing his daughter was undoubtedly taking a toll on his body. Five years seemed to have gone by in the recent days —new wrinkles plagued his forehead.

"After the wedding and what I did to Harkbin, I've taken solace in solitude. It helps me think clearly," the king said. "Fewer people approach me and ask me about what happens next when I isolate myself—hypothetically, at least."

"I understand," Kaine responded. "There's much to process. Much around us has changed, even among the markets. People are looking over their backs, keeping their distance from strangers, and doing anything they can to avoid endangering themselves. Some believe there are still Throatians among us and that they're hiding for now so they can sacrifice more people later."

The king gestured for Kaine to walk over to his large table nearby the throne and followed him there. Scribbled papers and diagrams of various sizes covered the mahogany surface. Presumably, the king had drawn out all the parchments during his days of sequestering himself.

"I've been cataloging all events surrounding the wedding," the king explained. "A lot is stirring up in the aftermath. I was hoping to get your opinion about the future."

"My opinion?" Kaine questioned. "I'm not sure I'm qualified to give a king advice, but I'll try my best."

"I meant to meet with Eisenbern earlier too, but I got distracted by something," Ether said. "You two were the only ones who tried to talk me out of killing Harkbin. You can't deny you were more willing to challenge me than most people about what happened. I need resistance from those nearby me to keep me in check, more than just soldiers who merely follow orders. This is only the beginning, and as we move forward, I don't want to lose my morality."

Kaine shook his head. "What can I do for you?"

"I'll be direct," Ether von Stonewall said, putting his hand on Kaine's shoulder. "Should I declare war on the Throatian Kingdom?"

Kaine balked at the question as the surrounding silence of the throne room pierced his ears.

"I'm… I'm definitely not qualified to decide that," Kaine said. "Morally, yes, perhaps we should declare

war, but I have no idea if we can defeat the Throatians, or at what cost. There are possible worldwide
ramifications regarding this choice."

"Your opinion alone isn't deciding what the
kingdom does," Ether said. "I just want to know your
thoughts."

"I need a moment, please," Kaine said. The king
nodded and let Kaine look over the maps and charts.

Hands clammy and slippery, Kaine picked up one
of the scattered papers from Ether's collection. The
parchment showed a simple three-column list of
potential allies, potential enemies, and unknowns.
First on the list of allies was the Leila Kingdom. The
unknowns list contained the Lucidian Enclave and
several other factions Kaine had never heard of before.

"I am certain I already have my answer, but I
need to know that my judgment hasn't been clouded," Ether added. "I made the mistake of letting fear
push me into marrying off my daughter. Despair led
me to killing Harkbin. Anger could carry me into an
even bigger set of problems."

Still holding the sheet of paper, Kaine stared over
at Ether's throne. The God Stones hidden within it
were perhaps the most dangerous piece of the
puzzle, especially if they ever entered a war. He
could not help but ask the king about them.

"About those... gold pieces... Lydia borrowed

from you," Kaine said, looking up at Ether. He gave the king a wink. "Did you confirm that they're back safely where they belong?"

The king paused momentarily to digest the question, then gave a slight nod. "Yes, I confirmed it myself. Weighed them too. Everything's as it should be now."

Kaine put the paper back down and studied another one, a map of the Darian Kingdom and all its lands. Across the sea was the Throatian Kingdom, an island circled by a thick red line. Was Ether planning to surround and capture it?

"The situation is delicate," Kaine noted, "yet it seems war is inevitable regardless of whether we start it. Retaliation for executing the Throatian royal family is unavoidable, and even if the Throatians don't care about that, a violent religion still dominates their country."

"Who could have foreseen that they would orchestrate an arranged marriage just to murder someone for magic?" Ether said.

"And why didn't they wait until they were back on their island to do it?" Kaine added. He held his tongue and didn't reveal that what had happened conflicted with what Lydia had originally told him. Sometime between the evening of the rehearsal dinner and the next day, the Throatians had changed

175

their plans, but it wasn't clear what advantage it had given them.

"The red armored knight," Ether said. "Maybe he was a spy or an informant. Everything was fine until he met us along the road. I haven't seen him since then, but I'm assuming he got paid the bag of coins for something he did to help the Asche family."

"He's probably not important. The more urgent matter is that Thane is still alive," Kaine added. "I doubt their religion will tell them to stay isolated on their island. Religion always spreads, regardless of its principles."

"Ramifications aside, do you believe we're justified in declaring war because of this?"

"Justified, indeed, but peace yet remains a possibility," Kaine said, sensing a reinvigoration of his noble upbringing and roots. "If the Throatian Kingdom takes initiative and condemns the Asche family's actions and their religion, I think we could remain neutral with the rest of their kingdom. Either way, I wouldn't put all of my trust in them ever again."

"I agree with you," Ether von Stonewall replied. "Seeing it from your perspective, without apology, the personal biases I have don't matter."

"But, have we received any word from Prince Thane?"

"Not yet. If a bird were on its way, it would have

arrived by now. Chances are an apology isn't coming. Thank you for everything, Kaine—I'll start preparing for this war."

Kaine nodded. "No need to thank me. My contribution was insubstantial."

The king laughed. "You're too humble, Kaine. You've been there all the times I needed you since Lydia first went missing. Which reminds me—I have another offer for you."

Kaine's stomach fluttered. "An offer, sir?"

"Yes, an alternative to being a retainer," Ether von Stonewall said. "The council and I can continue with that if you choose, or you can have a ranked position in the Darian Guard instead."

"Ranked position?" Kaine stammered. "I mean, I know how to use a sword, but I've never been a soldier before. There's my arm too; it's going to take a long time to recover."

"Your arm will heal eventually," Ether said. "You already proved your skills and that you can keep a level head under pressure. I need that when we go to war with the Throatian Kingdom. You'd probably get to work closely with your friend Eisenbern, too. What do you think? Will you take it?"

"My King," Kaine said, staring at the ground. "It would be my honor to serve you and the Darian Kingdom in any capacity you deem necessary. Still, as of now, I believe my strengths are best suited for

the retainer position. If I take on the retainer position and forgo the Darian Guard, would that be
acceptable?"

The king tilted his head curiously. "Are you sure?
I thought you'd choose the Darian Guard. Retaining
the prince and princess will satisfy you, but it may
bore you until they grow older. So, how about a
compromise?"

"What do you have in mind?"

"Start the retainer role for now while your arm
heals and bond with Xander and Kira. Whenever
you're healed, you'll join me in the war against the
Throatians. If we are careful and lucky, the conflict
won't even last six months. The Throatians live on a
relatively small island—it shouldn't be that hard to
conquer once we get the entire Darian Fleet out
there. If the war goes on longer than that, I'll send
you back home to be the retainer for Xander and
Kira early. How's the arrangement sound? Do we
have a deal?"

Once again, perhaps, Kaine had only the illusion
of choice, yet the offer seemed fair. If Kaine could
survive the war, his future would be secure. Traveling with the Darian Fleet was far safer than the
merchant ships he'd previously sailed on. He also
remembered that whenever he'd visited the Throatian island, their defenses had seemed lacking.
Chances were that once the Darian Fleet arrived at

the Throatians' island, a siege would start, and they'd cut off any supply routes. If the war played out that way, the Throatians would have no choice but to surrender, eventually.

"Count me in," Kaine said. "If we are careful and calculating enough, six months should be plenty of time to force a surrender."

The king nodded approvingly. "Excellent, Sir Khalia! That's the kind of morale we need. Go on ahead and rest for the day. Tomorrow, you'll give your retainer's oath to me in front of the council, and we'll announce the war to the public."

"Thank you for everything, my king," Kaine replied. "You've given me a chance at a new life. I appreciate it."

As Kaine ventured into the Darian capital's streets, he took in all the ordinary citizens going about their daily lives. There were so many people, shops, and genuinely peaceful routines thriving in the Darian capital. They were all worth protecting from the Throatians. Despite having his future laid out in front of him, the events of the past month still burned the back of his mind. Making peace with

Lydia and trying to put everything behind him was the only way for the next chapter of his life to begin.

"What are you hoping to buy today?" a florist asked as he approached her stall. "Our garden yields sunflowers, roses, daisies, orchids, and any other flowers you'd like."

"Just some roses, please," Kaine said.

The florist failed to hide her smirk. "I hope she accepts your apology. Roses usually work well for that."

"Pardon?"

"The only times I really sell roses aside from holidays is when men are apologizing to their girls for something," she informed with a wink. "That's why you're so anxious; I'm right, aren't I?"

"That's somewhat correct, I guess," Kaine said.

"Good luck to you then," the florist said. "Flawless red roses always work to resolve a fight."

"Thanks," Kaine said, desiring no further elaboration. He paid for the flowers and carried them out into the crowds of the buzzing market.

Holding the roses close to his chest, he took a deep breath and marched his way over to the graveyard. As he approached the princess's grave, he set the roses upon her tombstone. War was on the horizon now, and it was as inevitable as her sacrifice. He secured his coat as the wind blew around him.

"Nothing went right or as I'd hoped for, Lydia," he said to her. "You were afraid of a war against the Throatian Kingdom, but it seems nothing we could do would stop it from happening. I'm sorry I couldn't save you, but I'll try harder with Xander and Kira. Everything I can do to protect them, I'll do; I promise."

Gusts of wind blew the flowers off her grave, so he picked the roses up and set them back on again.

Though he'd only known Lydia for a few days, she'd changed his life forever. If Kaine hadn't met Lydia, he knew he'd still be scavenging around for valuable mushrooms in the forest as a commoner, unaware and unconcerned with news and politics affecting the world. He wished Lydia were still alive so she could see how much she'd positively affected his future by vetting him and persuading him to serve the king. The problem was that there wasn't enough time to ask her what he'd wanted to know about her or to thank her for everything she'd done.

Lydia was gone, and the bright future of their friendship faded with her passing. His fists tensed as he stared at her grave, but he quickly relaxed them when the breeze presented him with the scent of the fresh red roses. Kaine knew he could never forget the Wedding of the Torn Rose, for it had torn a piece of him too.

9

EPILOGUE

Upon his return to the chamber, Kaine discovered an unmarked letter subtly placed just within his doorway. The exterior of the envelope was unmarked and plain. An uncanny thrill went through him as he opened the generic wax seal and recognized the familiar handwriting of Lydia. Presumably for confidentiality, she must have sent the message beforehand, outside of the official delivery channels. Without delay, he read it:

Kaine Khalia,

It's important for you to know the truth, despite how much it scares me. I don't expect you to understand or believe everything I'm about to tell you, but someone advised me you might be the only person capable of accepting my true intentions.

You and I were being used for a higher purpose—something greater than we were aware of. Keep this in mind, and please don't resent me for what surrounded the wedding.

Much took place in the shadows we couldn't see. I warn you that a knight in crimson armor sits in the center of it all. Remember this, especially as the inevitable conflict between the kingdoms plays out. Besides the one I've known as my god, there's no enemy with stronger magic than him. Beware the knight—he thrives in chaos.

I failed to stop what's coming, but this greater threat infects all else around it. My mission is to help set things right again, so in the meantime, please protect the God Stones. Find a new location to hide them. We cannot risk them falling into the wrong hands, as I almost let them go. Everything depends on it. Whoever wields their magic determines the future. I regret I couldn't do more to prevent what happened, but it's clearer to me now that everything had to serve its purpose.

There's so much I regret, and so much I've lost, but this is only the beginning. Please forgive me for what I have set in motion. It's my fault for failing to stop it, but there's little else I could have done. I had all the wrong facts.

For now, remember me by this letter, and forget what you saw me do before. None of it matters because none of it was as it seemed. There's a considerable lot to achieve in order to defeat the darkness plaguing our world. A friend of mine—a powerful one—believes you will play an integral role in the greater war still to come. Kaine, I'm unable to determine the specifics yet, but I trust my friend is correct. Hold your heart close in the meantime and be ready when the time approaches.

THE SINGLE SHEET OF PARCHMENT FLUTTERED DOWN to Kaine's feet, then skittered across the floor. The handwriting, neat, small, and feminine in style, was just as he remembered from the letter he'd drunkenly burned before the wedding. But it couldn't be right. It had to have been Lydia who'd written the letter he'd just read. After all, she'd given the first letter to him and the penmanship was exactly the same. But the bottom of this second letter challenged what should have been a simple fact.

This new letter held one crucial detail that shifted his entire interpretation of the words. Lydia hadn't sent Kaine this latest message—though it would have been so much simpler if she had. Instead of finding the LVS initials at the bottom of the sheet as expected, Kaine saw the letters T and A. That single detail, resting quietly at the bottom of the page, made him question everything he thought he already knew.

Only one person he'd recently encountered had those initials.

Prince Thane Asche.

BOOK 2 CHAPTER PREVIEW

Next is a bonus preview chapter from Symphony of Crowns and Gods Book 2: Gravity of Obedience. This story begins months prior to Book 1 and moves forward, expanding on the events of Wedding of the Torn Rose. I hope you will enjoy this glimpse of the next part and what's coming later on in the series. To order Gravity of Obedience, please visit www. theauthorbrian.com or whichever storefront you purchased this book.

Thank you and enjoy!

— Brian A. Mendonça

GRAVITY OF OBEDIENCE
PREVIEW

Once White Boar's Landing closed itself off from foreign traders, the next months flew by. As the port turned approaching ships away, rumors of Throatian magic spread rapidly throughout the world. With the seeds of their lie flourishing, Harkbin sent King Ether von Stonewall a letter of introduction and asked to form an alliance by marriage. A messenger ship bearing the von Stonewall sigil—a golden sun spread across a maroon backdrop—brought the acceptance ten weeks later.

The wedding between the two nations would happen in six to eight weeks, depending on how long it would take the royal family to sail to Starlight Beach on the Yaenian continent. Harkbin and Urith collaborated with the Elders on the logistics of transporting three ships of Son See'ers to accompany them on the journey. The days passed quickly, and the time felt more like a week instead of months, which gave Thane little chance to come to terms with his fate. Despite those limitations, he spent as much time with Cereene as possible.

The morning he was supposed to leave for the Darian Kingdom, he prayed at the Temple of White and then trudged down the winding dirt pathway to her home.

"Cereene?" Thane called quietly as he neared her shack.

The sun had barely risen, and most of the Throatian people, scattered among the hills in their single-room stone huts, were still asleep. The trip to the Darian Kingdom was a mission in the service of Zann-Xia-Czul, so Harkbin had insisted that they abstain from a big celebration for the family. Aside from its complexity and urgency, Thane's father requested everyone treat their journey the same as any other religious task. The Asche family would quietly leave that morning and return more than a month later, depending on how the winds favored them.

"Shivanna Adul," Cereene said. "I'm ready for the hike. Do you need water before we go?"

"I'm okay for now," Thane replied. He took a satchel from her and strapped it around his back for later.

"Do you think we can complete the entire loop of the trail within an hour? You can't be late for your journey."

"We'll move at a quick pace."

An hour wasn't long enough, and it never would be. He wished he could stay with her indefinitely and that the problem of the sorceress didn't exist. This was their last opportunity to see each other while everything was still relatively calm. Thane had a strong suspicion that once he returned to their island with the princess, the assault from the sorceress would begin. His days were numbered, and there wouldn't necessarily be an opportunity to tie up his affairs later. For now, he was living as if he had a terminal illness. He would die, and such would be his end. While Thane had accepted the purpose of his sacrifice, the enigmatic circumstances surrounding it placed a constant weight on his chest.

His heart pounded as they trekked the trails of a smaller, unnamed mountain nestled near Mount Sephorr. Unlike the snow-filled peaks of the holy mountain, the adjoining ridges retained the tropical humidity of the rest of their island. Still, the air there was thin, and the breezes that wafted from where Zann-Xia-Czul concealed himself lent a chill to the atmosphere.

"It was a direct command from our god, but none of this feels right," Thane blurted out.

Cereene's footsteps came to a halt. As she cleaned the sweat from her forehead, Thane noticed several tears cascading down her cheeks.

"I couldn't find anything in the history or lore," Cereene said. "And if I can't save you from going, I want to come with you. The Darian Kingdom's capital has a very famous library. If I could spend some time there during your wedding—"

"We've gone over this. You can't join."

"I know, I know. I just… I wish I could."

"You don't understand Common Tongue. How would you read the books there?"

"Thane…"

Cereene's lip froze in place, and Thane couldn't tell if she was angry or sad. Slowly, he stepped forward and embraced her.

"I honestly wish I were to marry you instead," he said, "but I can't disobey Zann-Xia-Czul. Even though he knows everything, he still asked me to do this. It's the only way, even though none of it feels right."

"Nobody wants you to die," she insisted. "But I… I just want us to live."

"I know."

"I've never stopped praying for another means to fight the sorceress. And once you've returned here, I don't know how much longer—"

"You don't need to say it," Thane said, letting her

go. He nudged her gently, and they resumed walking again.

As they advanced towards the summit, the snowy landscape of Mount Sephorr stared down at them from across the valley. Tiny gray huts dotted the green hills between them, and castle-like Loyalty Circles punctuated the depth of the valley every mile or so. It all seemed insignificant from so far above, and Thane couldn't help but wonder how his life was somehow powerful enough to protect all of it.

"Do you think the Darians know of Zann-Xia-Czul?" Thane asked.

"You must have forgotten they worship Asura," Cereene said. "Still, maybe you can teach them about our god while you're there."

His eyes focused far down into the valley below, where minuscule Son See'ers were lining up outside Loyalty Circle Fourteen for their contributions. There was no escaping the Reminders of Suffering and Death. Thane wondered if only Throatians bred and sacrificed their own people in the name of their religion.

"I don't think it's a good idea," Thane said. He remembered Ibiram Lionheart, the foreign man he'd killed what only seemed like days ago. "Our beliefs differ from theirs. They'd never understand Loyalty Circles or Breeding Farms. That's been a part of my recent worries."

"Why is that?"

"It strikes me as odd that our religion is confined here, and nobody really ever comes or goes from our homeland," Thane said. "One's birth is the sole means of entering our island and understanding our culture. Death is the only way out. Perhaps we're wrong about some things."

"Having these conditions is certainly by design," Cereene said. Without a doubt, her loyalty to Zann-Xia-Czul overshadowed her true feelings about Thane's destiny. "Our god chose us to be his people, and we'll expand from here when he wills it."

They continued hiking, traversing their way down the several switchbacks on the opposite side of the hill. As the temperature rose, an empty sky offered no shield from the sun's relentless rays. If they stayed out too long, their skin would not darken—it would only burn.

"It all seems like such a waste," Thane said. "Breeding Farms are no different from animal farms. We grow people only for their blood and discard the rest of what makes them human. I can't understand why we think it's right when it's obviously so wrong. Zann-Xia-Czul needs blood to defend our island, but no other country lives as we do. Maybe our religion is why the sorceress wants to destroy us."

"You're overthinking it again," Cereene said. "It doesn't have to be so complicated. Sometimes things are simply how they're meant to be. That's the only explanation. You can't keep imagining ulterior motives, or you'll get trapped in an endless cycle of wondering what's true or false, with no way to verify any of it. You can't prove or deny the absolute intentions of a god's command."

The branches of a small, berry-filled bush reached across the trail, so Thane plucked some of its fruit. Each fuchsia berry, firm and smooth, rested in his palm as an offering. Cereene accepted one, and it crunched as she took her first bite.

"It's no different from fighting a war," she continued. "Other countries protect some of their people at the expense of others. They build armies to defend their lands or claim resources. People die for their kingdoms all the time and for many reasons. The only distinction between us and them is that Zann-Xia-Czul provides everything we need. Those who die in the Loyalty Circles serve a purpose; their deaths carry significance. We, the survivors, never forget about the deceased."

"The only differences between the Son See'ers and cattle are that they walk on two legs, and we don't eat them," Thane chided. "Many of our people don't even have names and are forgotten from the moment we sacrifice them. People only care about remembering those they knew."

"Stop it, Thane," Cereene said. "This shouldn't be my last memory of you."

He froze. "I'm sorry."

"It's fine."

They walked in silence, and Cereene lingered behind him the entire way back. Every time Thane looked over his shoulder, she glared down at her feet. By the time they finally arrived back at her home, it was time for Thane to go to White Boar's Landing and depart on his quest.

"It won't be easy for you to marry the Darian princess, knowing what's coming next," Cereene said. "But please, promise me that, no matter what, we can talk again after your return. I want to redo our final meeting."

"I'm sorry about today, Cereene," he said. "My mind is overwhelmed, and I'm struggling with discerning right from wrong. I—"

"I know that, but promise me this," Cereene said. "Promise me that today won't be the last time we meet."

READ NEXT: GRAVITY OF OBEDIENCE

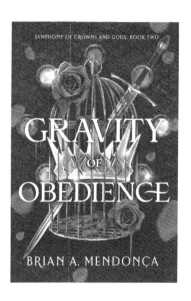

No one serves a god without paying the cost.

When his father disappears on a religious pilgrimage, Prince Thane is chosen to ascend a sacred mountain in a desperate attempt to find him, plunging him into a world of spiritual upheaval, divine conspiracies, and the terrifying prospect of a holy war.

There, he uncovers a harrowing warning: their god's protection from a sorceress hinges on unthinkable blood sacrifices, with Thane himself poised to be a primary offering. Bound by obedience and the terrifying demands of his god and family, Thane embarks on a journey that will challenge the very foundation of his faith and crown.

Racing against time, Thane must navigate the tumultuous world of royal politics and family conflicts to keep his homeland safe. Torn between his love for Cereene, his loyalty to his people, and the moral implications of their religion, Thane stands on the precipice of a decision that could shatter his world forever.

Everything changes when an invincible knight in crimson armor approaches, promising to tip the scales in a way Thane could have never imagined. Layers of deception unravel, and revelations emerge as a conflict extending beyond the realms of their island surfaces. With an eerie understanding of Thane's inner turmoil and an irresistible offer that reveals the true price of devotion, the knight makes it unclear who is really friend or foe. Thane's world spirals further into chaos as sacrifices become blurred and the signs of the long-anticipated war between gods grow louder.

Swept into the grandeur of royal weddings, hidden magic, and nefarious plots, the line between loyalty and disobedience blurs. The sacrifices demanded of him become unbearable, pushing Thane to question the very core of his beliefs, and bringing him face to face with an all-consuming choice. Will Thane obey the god who has orchestrated his life, or rebel against the gravity of obedience that will change the destiny of his people?

Prince Thane and Princess Lydia may be the only way of stopping the oncoming threat of the sorceress, but their marriage alone won't solve any of their problems.

Gravity of Obedience is the thrilling sequel to the Wedding of the Torn Rose.

BOOKS BY BRIAN A. MENDONÇA

<u>Symphony of Crowns and Gods Series</u>

Wedding of the Torn Rose (Book 1)

Gravity of Obedience (Book 2)

Prophecy of Tears and Sacrifice (Book 3)

Available at most major book retailers.

Store links can be found here: theauthorbrian.com

AN IMPORTANT NOTE FROM THE AUTHOR

As the creator of the Symphony of Crowns and Gods series, my primary aim is to transport readers like yourself on an unforgettable journey. This first book, *Wedding of the Torn Rose*, was designed to be shorter than the others, allowing you to swiftly decide if this is the type of narrative that resonates with your reading preferences.

I would love to hear your thoughts about it! If the book has captured your interest, would you kindly consider sharing your experience on platforms such as Amazon, Goodreads, BookBub, or any other convenient platform? A few words from you can guide fellow readers and significantly enhance the visibility of the series.

But more than that, your insights serve as my compass in this expansive landscape of storytelling. Your feedback and suggestions fuel my inspiration and aid me in weaving tales that deeply touch your heart.

Thank you in advance for your time and input. You are not just a reader; you are a vital part of my creative journey. And please remember, each review illuminates the path for the next grand adventure someone might embark upon in the Symphony of Crowns and Gods series.

Sincerely,
Brian A. Mendonça

To help, please visit:
https://www.theauthorbrian.com/review-request

Or use this QR code:

JOIN BRIAN A. MENDONÇA'S EMAIL NEWSLETTER

WHY SIGN UP?

It's simple: fans on this email list get my official updates before anyone else, including any other blogs and social media websites. Here's the news you can expect:

- Upcoming releases and previews of upcoming books
- An open dialog about my author journey
- Deals and sales
- Opportunities for ARCs (Advance Reader Copies)
- Info about fantasy books from other indie authors

Sign up link:

https://theauthorbrian.com/join-brians-newsletter

Or use this QR code:

Made in the USA
Las Vegas, NV
22 November 2023

81360428R00132